Fingerprints
of
GRACE

CARYN COLE

Fingerprints *of* GRACE

TATE PUBLISHING
AND ENTERPRISES, LLC

Published by Tate Publishing & Enterprises, LLC
127 E. Trade Center Terrace | Mustang, Oklahoma 73064 USA
1.888.361.9473 | www.tatepublishing.com

Tate Publishing is committed to excellence in the publishing industry. The company reflects the philosophy established by the founders, based on Psalm 68:11,

"The Lord gave the word and great was the company of those who published it."

Book design copyright © 2012 by Tate Publishing, LLC. All rights reserved.
Cover design by Nicole McDaniel
Interior design by Rtor Maghuyop

Published in the United States of America

ISBN: 978-1-62024-984-0
1. Fiction / Romance
2. Fiction / Sagas
12.07.03

Dedication

To all whose pain and brokenness has not gone
unnoticed, but has become of great value.
May you dare to dream again.

Chapter 1

"*Lizzy, wait up a minute!*"

Lizzy's heart skipped a beat when she heard her name. She stopped and slowly turned her head to see if the voice matched the person she hoped it would be.

"*Do you mind if I walk with you for a bit?*"

"*No, not at all!*" *she answered, blushing. This was what she had been longing for ever since they had first met a few weeks ago.*

"*Where are you headed?*" *he asked with a smile as he cocked his head slightly.*

"*Nowhere in particular. It's such a beautiful day; I don't want to go home.*"

"*Would you like to take a walk in the park? Maybe some of the others will be there too.*"

"*Sure!*" *she replied eagerly as they turned and headed toward the park.*

The warmth of the sun felt good on this spring day. New leaves were forming on the trees, and the grass was beginning to green up from winter. As they approached the park, voices could be heard in every direction. There were children playing on the playground, people walking their dogs, couples strolling hand in hand, and others just sitting on park benches soaking up the warmth.

"Look over there," said Mitch. "There's Butch, Peggy, and some of the others."

He turned toward them and waved. "Hello!" he shouted. "Do you mind if we join you?"

Butch beckoned them with a wave of his hand. "Come on," he called to them.

Lizzy knew the others from school. She was just finishing her junior year of high school and would be graduating next year. It was at Peggy's party a few weeks ago that she had been introduced to Mitch.

"Anybody up for a game of football?" Michael asked hopefully as he drew the football out from behind his back. His blue eyes sparkled beneath a head of tousled blonde hair.

"Sure, count me in," Mitch answered, eager to play. He was a lighthearted sort of guy always up for a game.

"That makes four," counted Sammy. "What are we waiting for? Let's go!" The boys moved over to an open grassy area and soon had a serious game going between the four of them. Peggy, Carolyn, and Trisha scooted over to make room on the park bench for Lizzy.

"I saw you two looking at each other," Peggy teased. "How long has this been going on?"

"How long has what been going on?" asked Lizzy.

"You know, you and Mitch."

"This is the first time I've seen him since your party when you introduced us. We just ran into each other a few minutes ago before we came to the park, and that's all there is to it."

"Well, we'll wait and see what develops," said Carolyn. "I agree with Peggy—I saw how you two were looking at each other."

Lizzy's heart started beating faster. Now she knew it wasn't just her imagination, the others saw it too. She liked the way Mitch looked at her and had been hesitant to let her emotions run too fast with her heart. It's been two years since he graduated from high school. What can he possibly see in a girl still a month away from turning seventeen?

After spending several hours in the park, the group began to break up, and one by one they left until only Lizzy and Mitch remained.

"I guess I'd better be getting home too," Lizzy said as she started to gather her things.

"When can I see you again?" Mitch asked as he stooped down to help her. She looked up, and as their eyes met, her heart melted. It was all she could do to look into his gaze. Words wouldn't come. After a long pause, he said, "How about we start with you telling me where you live."

No, he couldn't come to the house and meet her mother. She wouldn't approve of her having a boyfriend, especially one so much older than her. Suddenly she found her voice. "Why don't we just meet somewhere instead?"

"Okay. Let's meet here tomorrow afternoon at one o'clock. How about over there on the bench by the water fountain."

"Okay. See you tomorrow," she said as they stood up at the same time.

Lizzy woke up with a start and looked around the room to get her bearings. She shuddered as she walked to the kitchen to fix her morning cup of hot tea.

"Where did that come from?" she said audibly. *After all these years and I'm dreaming about Mitch? I can think of better ways to wake up from a deep sleep.*

Her thoughts drifted back in time as she got dressed for work. Twenty years had passed since she'd first met Mitch at that party at Peggy's house. After her breakfast, she put her dishes aside on the counter to wash later. Still pondering this morning's dream, she opened her front door and drank in the warmth of the sunshine as she headed to work. As the day wore on, her thoughts faded from the dream to anticipation of the weekend at Haleub Place.

Gil, the groundskeeper at Haleub Place, met her at the station to drive her to her uncle's home. "Miss Lizzy, it's so good to see you again."

"You too, Gil," she replied.

"Anna, Ellen, and Kate have been busy all week preparing for this celebration," Gil said, shaking his head in amazement.

"It's exciting, isn't it, Gil, to see Marcus all grown up and about to graduate from college. Ten years ago, I would never have dreamed that any of this could happen."

"Has it been that long?" Gil reached up and scratched his head. "I remember the day I met Marcus. He showed up with a small tattered suitcase asking for a job and a place to stay. There's something special about that boy, Lizzy, something special."

The drive to Haleub Place went quickly as Gil and Lizzy reminisced over the strides Marcus had taken in the last few years.

"Ah, Lizzy. Congratulations on your son graduating from college!" Marshall said as he stepped out the front door onto the wide porch and gave her a big hug.

"It's me that should be congratulating you for all that you have poured into Marcus since he came to live with you," Lizzy replied.

"Come on in. Since you're the first one here, you have your choice of rooms. Kate has worked hard on getting all the rooms ready. We'll have a full house by tomorrow night." Marshall's deep brown eyes danced with excitement as he anticipated the arrival of all their guests. "Thank you, Gil," he said to the silver-haired gentleman as he set Lizzy's suitcase on the porch. "I'll take it from here."

As Lizzy and her uncle stepped inside the house, Anna met them in the hallway carrying a tray with tall glasses of lemonade and a basket full of her famous orange pecan muffins, still warm from the oven.

"I'll set this tray down here in the parlor for you two," she said and then turned to give Lizzy a warm hug. "We're all so excited about tomorrow. What an exciting day! Our Marcus, all grown up and finished with college. It seems like only yesterday that he came to live with us at Haleub Place."

"Yes, the time has gone by quite quickly hasn't it?"

Anna was all smiles as she turned to leave the room. Her white hair was gathered in a bun on the top of her head, and her apron covered most of her short body as she was not much more than five feet tall. "Ellen and I are almost done in the kitchen with the preparations for tomorrow. I'd better get back there to help out. See you in the morning," she said as she puttered down the hall humming to herself.

Lizzy chose an upstairs room with a view overlooking the flower gardens behind the house. In the distance stood rows of apple, pear, and plum trees, but the light was growing dim and only revealed shadowy shapes of gray. She would be able to see more clearly in the morning. It had been a long day, and she wasted no time in pulling back the covers of the bed. As she lay her head down on the pillow, her thoughts drifted back to the dream she had so rudely awakened from that morning. Why now, after all these years, would she dream of Mitch? They hadn't been married but a few months before he started staying out all night with no explanation. One night he stayed out all night and never came back. It was only a few weeks later when she had discovered that she was carrying his child.

At age fifteen, Lizzy's father died, leaving only her and her mother to carry on alone. The anger she felt at losing someone she had loved so dearly soon turned to rebellion. She started hanging out with the wrong crowd, and it was here that she had met Mitch through some mutual friends. She turned eighteen the year she graduated from high school and moved out abruptly, leaving no forwarding address for her mother. She and Mitch married with no ceremony, only a trip to the courthouse.

For years, Lizzy struggled to support herself and her son, Marcus. He was left with one family after another while she worked, until one day something inside her snapped. She had lost her job through no fault of her own and just couldn't face another day. She didn't even go pick up her son that day. Shame and regret kept her from going home to her mother, and she reasoned that Marcus would be better off with a "real" family than with her. By the time she came to her senses, the family had moved away, leaving no trace of Marcus.

These had been lean years for Lizzy, and if she had the choice, she'd rather not remember them. The past ten years had been like night and day in comparison. Her life turned around when she realized that she had family that loved her and cared about her no matter what. Somehow, knowing that people loved her gave her a reason for living. When her thinking changed, her life changed.

Marshall and Lizzy left early the next morning to go pick up Emelia, his late wife's sister, on the way to the college. The graduation ceremony would be held at one o'clock that afternoon. Gil, Anna, Ellen, and Kate would be coming up together a little later in a separate car.

Kings College was a small school nestled in the rolling green hills of the town of Springfield. It was only about two hours away from Haleub Place, so Marcus had been able to make several trips home over the past four years of school. With Lizzy's permission, Uncle Marshall had become her son's legal guardian as well as his surrogate father. Marcus thrived under his care and guidance as he poured into him what would have been passed on to his son if he and his wife had had children of their own.

Emelia was ready to go when Lizzy and Marshall arrived. She grabbed her walking cane, and they helped her to the car.

"I'm so excited to see our boy about to graduate! And just think, ten years ago, I didn't even know that I had a grandson!"

Emelia's deteriorating health had not affected her love of people one bit. Her mind was as sharp as ever and she loved children of all ages. It had taken some time, but she and Lizzy had mended their mother/daughter relationship and at present were on the best of terms.

"Marshall, you've done a wonderful job with Marcus."

"I agree!" chirped Lizzy from the back seat.

"It doesn't take much, when you start with exceptional ability," he replied.

"You gave him opportunities I could never offer, and I can't thank you enough, Uncle Marshall."

"The pleasure was mine," he replied modestly.

The next two hours passed quickly as they chatted all the way to Springfield, anticipation building as they drew closer to the school. They all shared this milestone as if it was their own.

Chapter 2

Marcus took a deep breath and sighed as he finished packing the last box. The few remaining clothes, bedding items, and personal articles would go in his suitcase tomorrow. A quick survey of the room revealed two twin beds and two wooden study desks with matching, sturdy chairs. The books that once lined the shelf above each desk were now in boxes. The room that just two days ago was full of life now seemed very empty.

Nathan, Marcus's roommate, had moved out two days ago after his last final exam. He was only a junior and had not planned on staying for the graduation ceremony. Both boys promised to keep in touch with each other as they said their good-byes. Nathan would be coming back in the fall for his senior year, but Marcus was not sure where the next year would take him.

These past four years had raced by so quickly, and now he was on the eve of graduation. What had happened to that timid boy that had never really belonged anywhere or had any family that cared about him? Tomorrow there would be several carloads of people driving in just to help him celebrate this milestone in his life. What a different path his life had been on since he came to Haleub Place.

Marcus lay awake in bed for a long time that night. Final exams were over, the packing was done, and he was alone with his thoughts. There had been something gnawing at him for a long time. Although he was grateful for all that his uncle had done for him in taking him in, bringing his family back together and seeing to his education, there was still something very much on his mind. He had a burning desire to find his father. Where did he live? Why did he leave? What was he like? What would his reaction be to knowing that he had a son? Marcus did not fully comprehend why, but not knowing the answer to these questions was like being held captive to the unknown. Without knowing his past, he could not fully comprehend his future. Before his eyelids closed, giving way to sleep, Marcus determined in his mind that he would search for his father just as Uncle Marshall had searched until he found his mother.

The sun rose bright the next morning, waking Marcus with its light. This was his big day; the spotlight would soon be on him. It was two hours before his family and friends of the family would be arriving to share in this celebration.

Marcus was graduating with honors. He had always been a quick learner, and once Uncle Marshall had taken an interest in his studies and set him on the right track, he flourished. Upon graduation, Marshall had offered to teach him the family business.

His thoughts were interrupted by a knock on the door. It was Charlie, a fellow classmate from down the hall.

"Would you like to join us for breakfast this morning?" he asked. "There are four of us left on the hall, and it will probably be our last meal together."

"Sure!" Marcus said with a quick nod of his head. "Thank you for asking," he said as he put his shoes on and grabbed his keys.

The air was warm and pleasant with a slight breeze. Flowers were in bloom all over the grounds, and all the trees were showing their green leaves. It was a beautifully cared-for campus, and Marcus felt sure that Mr. Thompson would approve.

The boys made their way past the other buildings to the dining hall.

"What a perfect day for an outdoor graduation," remarked Charlie.

"Yes, it is perfect," agreed Marcus.

Dan held the door open as the boys filed into the building for the last time. Hanging in the air was the familiar smell of eggs, sausage, potatoes and biscuits. One by one they filled their plates and sat down at the round table.

"So, Greg, what are your plans after today?" asked Charlie as they began to eat.

"Next week, I start as a teller at a bank in my hometown. It gets my foot in the door, and if I work hard, I'm sure that with time, promotion will come."

"I wish I had something sure like that waiting for me," Dan added. "Come Monday, I'll be out looking for a job. At least after today I'll have a degree to add to my resume. These last four years ought to count for something."

"What will you be doing, Charlie?" asked Marcus.

"A friend of my father said he had an opening in his business and to come look him up when I get home. Like Greg, I'll be starting off at the bottom but hope to build on that with time. Do you have any prospects, Marcus?" he asked.

Marcus had his mouth full when the question was asked so he had some time to think before his reply. He had caught the word *father* when Charlie answered, and it had sent his thoughts once again to his father. After swallowing, he replied.

"My uncle offered to teach me the family business when I graduated, and I plan on taking him up on his offer."

"Well, a toast to our futures!" Charlie said as he lifted his glass of orange juice.

The others joined in the toast with their glass in hand. After breakfast, the boys walked back to their dormitory building and parted ways to their rooms to take care of last-minute packing details. Soon, the parents and other guests would be arriving.

Marcus sat by the open window in his room, listening to the birds sing and chirp in the nearby maple tree. He was packed, ready, and just waiting for the first arrival. His mind had drifted back to thoughts of his father… and just how was he going to find his father anyway?

His thoughts were disturbed by the sound of voices in the hallway, followed by a knock on his door. He opened the door to find his mother and Uncle Marshall standing in the hallway.

"Hello, Mother," he said as she stepped in the room and gave him a big hug.

"Hello, Uncle Marshall," he said as his uncle shook his hand and gave him a big hug as well.

"Congratulations!" they both said together.

"We left Emelia sitting downstairs in the lobby so she wouldn't have to climb the stairs," Marshall told Marcus.

"Well, there's nothing keeping me up here," he said as he glanced back at his room. "Let's all go downstairs to the lobby." He led the way down the stairs. "You must have left really early this morning to get Grandmother before you drove over here."

"Marcus! Congratulations! This is your big day today," Emelia said as soon as she saw her grandson come around the corner.

"Thank you, Grandmother," he said as he leaned over to give her a kiss and a hug. "Don't get up. We've come to sit with you for a bit."

"Gil and the others should be here soon," said Marshall. "I told them to meet us here at the dormitory so we could all go sit together. The Bentons and the Trembleys said they would meet up with us after the ceremony."

"We're all here to celebrate with you, son," his mother said, beaming.

Their relationship had been rocky for a number of years and even non-existent at one point, but in their reunion, they had allowed forgiveness to give them a new start. Lizzy would never get those early years back, but she could take advantage of the time she had now.

Gil, Anna, Ellen, and Kate arrived within the hour, and after they all greeted Marcus they headed over to the graduation area so they could get seated together. Marcus stayed with them for a while and then excused himself in order to get lined up with his classmates for the graduation ceremony.

Kings College colors were reflected in the colors of the robes. All the girls were dressed in white and the boys in royal purple. Only the tassels had the two colors displayed together. They all had worked hard these past four years, and soon they would reach that bittersweet moment. They had achieved their goals but now had to say good-bye to those they had grown so close to. This chapter was almost over and soon a new one would begin for each of them. What once were goals would now become mileposts marking their journey.

As the music began, the graduates began to file into the seats marked off at the front of the assembly. The lawn at Kings College had been neatly manicured to accommodate all the chairs that had been set up for the occasion. Solos were sung and speeches delivered before the names were called one by one in alphabetical order.

With a last name beginning with *W*, Marcus had grown accustomed to being one of the last to be called, and today was no exception. "Marcus Reston Williams, with honors," resonated over the loudspeaker system. Emelia and Lizzy looked at each other as tears of joy began to well up in their eyes. There was not a dry eye among them, even Marshall was caught brushing his cheek with his hand. Anna and Gil were considered part of the family as well as Ellen and Kate. Anybody having any connection with Haleub Place was automatically considered family.

As Marcus walked across the stage to receive his diploma, his thoughts drifted back to the day he had found out that Mr. Jules was his great-uncle and Emelia was his grandmother. He was tempted to pinch himself now, as he did that day so long ago, to make sure that he wasn't dreaming. In just a few short years, he had transformed from a nameless nobody to a graduate with honors. Marcus was very grateful that the honors did not require him to make a graduation speech.

With the ceremony officially over, the graduates were now free to join their families out on the lawn.

"Congratulations!" chorused Gil and Anna together as they gave Marcus a big hug. "Well done, son. Well done!"

Ellen and Kate were next in line to offer their congratulations and hugs. Kate and Marcus were only a few years apart and had grown quite fond of each other over the years. He had become a big brother to her and she looked up to and admired him very much.

"Marcus! Congratulations!" a man's voice sounded from behind. He turned to find the Benton family gathered behind him. Winston was a business associate of Mr. Jules and, when possible, often brought his family with him to Haleub Place.

"A job well done, Marcus!" said Jake, their twenty-four-year-old son. He had graduated from college two years earlier and was now in medical school working in research. He and Marcus hadn't seen each other much in the past few years as they had both been away at school in opposite directions.

"Hi, Kate!" cried Julia. She and Kate were good friends and always glad for an opportunity to spend some time together. "I'm glad we're coming to stay at Haleub Place for a few days. We have a lot to catch up on, especially since we both graduated from high school this year."

"Hello, everybody," sounded another familiar voice behind them. "Where's our graduate?" exclaimed Ben.

"He's over there talking to Jake," answered Kate. "Did Jonathan come with you?"

"Yes, he's with Lily over there," he said, pointing to his wife and son. "They're trying to make their way through the crowd. We got separated from one another in the middle aisle."

"Oh, I see them now," Kate said as she eagerly caught their attention with a wave.

Marshall made his way over to greet the Bentons and the Trembleys. "So glad you could make it to Marcus's graduation ceremony," he said warmly.

"Oh, we wouldn't have missed this. It's too important," replied Winston Benton.

"I second that," said Ben Trembley.

"As soon as we get Marcus's things loaded up, we're headed back to Haleub Place for the family celebration," said Marshall. "Gil brought Anna, Ellen, and Kate, and they should be the first ones to arrive home."

"Do you think they would have room for Julia?" asked Marjorie. "She'd love to ride back with Kate. You know how those two are when they get together," she said, chuckling.

"I'm sure that wouldn't be a problem. I'll say something to Gil. Perhaps Marcus would like to take Julia's place and ride back with you. That would give him and Jake some time together," said Marshall. "I'll mention it to him and see what he says."

"I'll give you a hand loading up his luggage," offered Winston.

"Thank you. I think I'll take you up on your offer. Many hands make quick work."

Marshall made his way through the throng of people to Gil and then to Marcus. Gil nodded in agreement to the plan for Julia to ride with them.

"Marcus, why don't we start loading up your things so we can get going soon? Winston has offered to help us."

"Sure thing, Uncle Marshall," he answered.

"By the way, Julia is riding back with Kate, which leaves an opening in the Benton's car. Don't feel you need to ride back with us if you'd rather spend some time with Jake on the way home."

"Are you sure you wouldn't mind?"

"No, not at all. This celebration is for you. This is your day! I expect your grandmother will probably fall asleep on the way home anyway. The day is far from over and she could use the rest."

Gil, and the ladies riding with him, were the first ones to leave for Haleub Place. They had some last-minute preparations to do before everyone arrived, and Julia had volunteered to help in any way she could.

Ben Trembley offered to help with Marcus's things also, so the four men headed to the dormitory to get the job done. Jake stayed with the others as he was physically challenged when it came to heavy lifting. They took their time as they leisurely strolled in the direction of the parking lot. In no time, the men had Marcus's things loaded and everyone headed in the direction of Haleub Place.

Chapter 3

Kate and Julia chattered all the way home to Haleub Place. The girls only saw each other a few times a year, and when they did, they were practically inseparable.

"So, Julia, what are you doing now that you've graduated from high school?" asked Kate.

"Well, next week I'm going to my grandparents' to spend a couple months with them over the summer. They are a lot of fun, and I like being with them whenever I can." She watched the scenery out the window for a while and then turned to Kate.

"What are you doing? Any plans?"

"No," said Kate wistfully, "just helping out my mother and Anna."

Julia turned to look out the window again then suddenly turned back to Kate. "What if you could come with me and spend the summer at my grandparents'?"

"Do you think I could?" asked Kate eagerly.

"I'll ask Mother after dinner tonight. I don't think it would be a problem for you to come with me. My grandparents would love you. Who wouldn't love you?!"

"Oh, this is exciting," Julia said about to burst with anticipation. "I can't wait to ask mother."

Ellen glanced over at her daughter sitting next to her. She and Anna had been talking over all the details of what they were going to do first when they got home. She'd heard the girls' excitement over something and paused to listen to them a minute.

"What's so exciting?" she interrupted.

"Julia's going to ask her mother if I can spend the summer with her at her grandparents'. Would that be okay with you if she said yes?" Her big blue eyes looked longingly at her mother, waiting for a positive response.

"I don't see why not, if it's okay with her parents and grandparents."

"Oh, thank you, thank you, thank you!"

Kate and Julia looked at each other, hardly able to contain their excitement. Gil chuckled to himself as he heard the girls' plans. He was a good listener and had been following both conversations on the drive home. No one had addressed him directly in either conversation, and he was content to leave it that way and let them do all the talking.

"Why don't you sit up front with Marshall, if you don't mind? I feel a nap coming on, and I'll probably be more comfortable in the backseat. You two can talk, and it won't disturb me a bit."

Lizzy helped her mother get settled in the backseat, using some of the bedding and pillows from Marcus's luggage for her to lean against. Soon everybody was settled in the other three cars and ready to go. Marshall pulled out first and the Bentons and Trembleys followed. All the guest rooms would be full tonight with all the adults as well as their children. They hadn't been driving long when Lizzy glanced to the back seat and saw that her mother was sleeping soundly. She had been gazing out the window lost in her thoughts, savoring the moments of the day and anticipating the evening celebration for her son. Lizzy cherished the times with her uncle. He was full of wisdom and always had a way of setting her at ease. Even his voice was deep and mellow with a reassuring warmness to it. She turned to him and began to share her thoughts.

"I woke up from the strangest dream yesterday morning. Of all people, I dreamed about when I first met Mitch, Marcus's father."

"Was it a pleasant dream?" he inquired as he glanced toward her.

"The dream was pleasant enough, but the thought of dreaming about him wasn't. He deserted me! He lied to me!"

"It's only natural that an occasion of this sort would stir up thoughts of him. Most students have both parents present for their children's graduation, and I'm sure even with all of us who came to help Marcus celebrate, that you felt the stigma of a not-so-normal family arrangement. It's okay to acknowledge the differences as long as you know that you and Marcus are loved and that these differences in no way serve as roadblocks to your individual identities or destinies."

"Why does your subconscious mind address things that your conscious mind doesn't?"

"That's a deep question, Lizzy," her uncle replied. "I can't answer the why, I only know that the mind, body, and emotions all work together to bring wholeness to each of us. Perhaps there are still things to be dealt with concerning Mitch. You've mended your relationships with your mother, Marcus, and me, but you never had a chance for closure with Mitch. You can only be responsible for your own decisions and their consequences, not someone else's.

"From what you told me, Mitch never knew that you were pregnant. You can't hold him accountable for not helping you with a son he never knew about. You surmised that he walked out on you, and that may be true, but the fact is that you really don't know what happened, or even if he is still alive."

Marshall was silent for a moment and then continued. "You mentioned that he lied to you. Do you want to talk about that?"

"He said that he loved me, but he would tell me things that later I found out were untrue. After a while, I didn't believe anything he said because I couldn't trust his word."

"It's hard to learn to trust again," her uncle added, "after you've built up walls to protect yourself. Do you think you could let go of any hurt or anger that you might have held on to? It's not hurting him, it's only hurting you."

Lizzy turned her head toward her uncle. "How do I do that?"

"Take responsibility for the choices you've made and the paths they led you down. Don't live in the past with any 'what ifs.' Move forward with today—from this day forward. There are no regrets for tomorrow, only possibilities."

Lizzy leaned back on the headrest and closed her eyes. She was silent for a while as she let her uncle's words sink in. "The fact that I was hesitant to let Mitch come to the house and meet my mother should have been my first clue. Only questionable things are kept in the dark; there's no reason to hide good things. I chose to hang out with the wrong crowd and ignored and even hurt those who did love me. I chose to turn my back on the truth of who really loved me, and believed the lies instead."

Shifting in her seat, she stretched her legs and let out a sigh. She looked straight ahead and with a quick nod of her head said, "You're right. I can't hold Mitch responsible for all my struggles in taking care of Marcus. I had options, but I chose not to take advantage of them. If you hadn't come looking for me, I'd still be stuck in my regrets and disconnected from my family. I owe a lot to you," she said as she turned back to her uncle. "Thank you for caring enough to search for me and pull me back into the family."

Marshall glanced over at her as he kept driving. "Lizzy, that's what family is all about, caring for each other no matter what, through lean times as well as times of joy and plenty. We all plant seeds through our actions as well as our words. When the harvest comes in, we find that we reap what we have sown, both good and bad."

Lizzy answered abruptly, "I pray that I have crop failure on the bad seeds I've sown."

Chuckling at her honesty, her uncle continued, "Forgiveness brings crop failure when bad seeds are sown; you've done that Lizzy. Look at the harvest of friends and family relationships you have now. You are blessed and so are we."

Lizzy reflected on all the ways she had been blessed in the last ten years. She was ready to let go of Mitch and the past and move forward with no regrets. The past twenty-five years had had its ups and downs, but the last ten years had taught her how to cope with past mistakes and actually learn from them. It was a big step, but Lizzy was finally ready to say that she was thankful for the past because of the lessons she had learned from those experiences.

Emelia stirred as she attempted to change positions on the bedding and pillows in the back seat.

"Are you okay, Mother?" Lizzy asked as she turned to check on her mother.

"Yes, dear," she said as her eyes fluttered open.

"We're almost there, Emelia, about half an hour away," Marshall added.

"Well, I feel rested after that sound sleep. What a wonderful day it's been. Lizzy, I wish your father could have seen his grandson walk across that stage today."

Lizzy smiled, "I wish he could have too, Mother."

This was the first time in years that she'd heard her mother make mention of her father. In the past, the mention of his name had always upset Lizzy, so her mother had been careful not to mention him when she was around.

"How does it feel to have four years of college behind you, Marcus?" said Mr. Benton as they drove away from the campus.

"It doesn't seem like such a long time now as I'm looking back, but there were times when I thought I'd never see the end," Marcus replied.

"I know what you mean," added Jake. "After four years of college and two years of graduate school behind me, I have two more years of graduate school to go, but at least I'm three fourths of the way through."

"You sure have a lot of determination, Jake," said Marcus.

"Thanks, it's really not that hard because I get to do a lot of research in the areas I'm really interested in."

"And what is it that you're interested in?"

"The area I was studying this past semester was trying to unlock the cause of birth defects. What goes wrong in the DNA coding from two healthy people to cause a deformity or disability like mine when I had to wear leg braces as a child?"

"That sounds fascinating, Jake. I'm glad you are getting to do what you love."

"I saw in the program today that your major was in business. What are your plans now?"

"Uncle Marshall offered to teach me the family business when I finished school. I'm ready to take him up on his offer now. It would be great if I could get to travel with him as well."

"You'll meet a lot of interesting people, like when you met us." Jake beamed with a silly grin.

"I remember the first day I met you and your sister, Julia. I was shy back then and had never really had a friend. I'm so glad that Mr. Thompson encouraged me to catch up with you, Julia, and Kate. That was the first time I ever had fun with someone close to my own age."

"Speaking of Kate, is something going on between you two?" asked Jake.

"I'd like for there to be something going on, but Kate's been like a sister to me for the past ten years. I like her a lot, and I don't want to mess up our relationship if she doesn't want to be more than a sister. I care about her too much for that to happen."

"I'll get with Julia on that," he offered. "Chances are that Kate tells her everything anyway."

"Thanks, Jake. I'd really appreciate that."

As soon as they arrived, Gil, Anna, and Ellen went right to work getting the final preparations done for the celebration.

"You girls can help in the kitchen," Ellen told her daughter and Julia. "There are some extra aprons hanging up near the door if you need one."

"Thanks," said Julia. "It sure smells good in here."

"Anna and my mother have been cooking for days. Now we finally get to eat the goodies." Kate licked her lips. "I've had my eye on those cherry pies since yesterday."

"I bet you are a good cook too, by now."

"Mother let me make these cookies over here. They are pecan sandies, one of my favorites."

"I can't wait until the others get here," Julia said as she eyed all the food in the kitchen. "All this is making me very hungry."

"Why don't you girls start taking some of these dishes out to the big serving table in the dining room," called Ellen over her shoulder. "We'll set out the hot and cold items when everybody arrives, but all the other things like muffins, pies, cookies, and the like can go out now."

The two girls began taking the food out from the kitchen, sniffing each dish as they set it down on the long buffet table set up for the occasion. Soon all the preparation was done and the family and guests began arriving. The wide front porch had been set up with small tables to accommodate everyone. When all had gathered, Marshall stood by the front door to address the gathering.

"Thank you all so very much for coming to the graduation ceremony and to this celebration that we're having here today. Marcus, you have inspired all of us with your hard work and determination over the years, but especially these last four years. Congratulations, son! You've done a fine job, and we are honored to know you."

Marshall started clapping and everyone joined in a round of applause. Marcus blushed a bit at all the attention, but arose from his seat to attempt to speak. A bit choked with emotion, he began haltingly.

"Thank you all very much for coming today to share this celebration with me. All of you have had a part in getting me to where I am today, a graduate. You took me in…you loved me…encouraged me…and supported me. Thanks doesn't seem to be a big enough word to cover all that. I couldn't have done it without you." He slowly surveyed the group gathered before him, nodding to each one in acknowledgement of their love and support of him.

"Thank you again for all you've done for me, and thank you especially for coming out today." With that, Marcus sat down and reached for his glass of lemonade and took a swallow to quench his thirst.

Anna rose from her seat on the porch bench. "All the food is ready. Please help yourself to the buffet laid out in the dining room. There's plenty to go around for everyone."

Marshall stood and heartily encouraged everyone, "Anna and Ellen have been cooking for days. Please, let's go eat!"

No further coaxing was necessary and all soon filed into the dining room and returned to the porch with plates loaded with delicious delectables. Herb roasted chicken, creamy mashed potatoes, home-grown green beans, and fresh-baked rolls were among the favorites. Cakes, pies, muffins, and cookies covered the dessert table, each one more tempting than the other. Conversation drifted from one table to another as everyone tried to catch up on the latest happenings in each family. It had been a full day for all of them and evening was coming on.

The first to turn in for the night was Emelia. "Good night, everyone!" she called out. "It's been a lovely day spent with lovely people. I'm not as young as the rest of you, so I need my beauty sleep. Sleep well, and I'll see you in the morning."

Lizzy helped her mother to her room on the first floor and made sure she had everything she needed before returning to the gathering on the porch. Marcus, Jake, Kate, and Julia all excused themselves to go down to the pond. The four of them had forged a close bond over the years and hadn't all been together since the previous summer.

Anna began to yawn. "Well, you'll have to excuse me too. The excitement of the day has begun to catch up with me. Good night to you all," she said as she turned to go inside.

"I'll help put everything away in the kitchen," added Ellen.

"The food was delicious, as usual," exclaimed Marjorie.

"Yes, it was," chorused those left on the porch.

Gil rose to make his exit, leaving only the Trembleys, Bentons, Lizzy, and Marshall.

"What a perfect ending for a perfect day." Lizzy sighed as she repositioned herself in her chair. "Good friends and family and good food have filled me up, and I am privileged to know each of you."

"It's our pleasure to know you and your son," remarked Winston.

"Thank you," she replied, smiling.

Soon others began to yawn as well and everyone stood up and said good night as they headed to their rooms.

Chapter 4

That night as he stretched out on the bed, Marcus laid his head back to rest on his clasped hands on his pillow. He was home. This was his home. Sometimes his mind wandered to the overwhelming reality that, in time, someday this might all belong to him. Marcus rested in the fact that his uncle Marshall would see that he learned all he needed to know to keep Haleub Place running. With school completed and graduation behind him, he was eager to start learning the family business. He had met many interesting people that had come to Haleub Place on business, but he had never had opportunity to travel with his uncle.

Over the years, Mr. Thompson had taught him how to care for the grounds and upkeep of the place, and he had been more than willing to help out in any way that he could. Haleub Place was known for its beautiful flower gardens and orchards as well as a vegetable garden with abundant produce.

Lizzy was the first to leave as she had to catch the train to be back at work the next day. The Bentons arranged to stay a day longer to give Kate some time to pack her things and travel back home with them. Julia's grandparents were excited about the girls coming for the summer. The Trembleys were leaving after dinner and traveling home that evening. Marshall would take his sister-in-law home when all the guests had left. She loved being with everyone and was in no hurry to get home.

The next day the Bentons piled into the car and good-byes were said. Anna and Ellen headed back to the kitchen.

"I'll clean the rooms, Anna, while you see to the kitchen. It's going to be awful quiet around here this summer without Kate." Ellen sighed as she wiped away a tear and smoothed her hair.

Gil was already in the garden as he liked to work in the cool of the morning before the heat of the day set in. Marcus had spent time with Julia, Jake, and Kate that morning.

"Remember," Marcus whispered to Jake so no one else could hear, "let me know what you find out about Kate."

"You've got my word on it. I'll let you know when I find something out. It shouldn't be that hard since she'll be staying with us for a week before she and Julia go to my grandparents." Jake winked at Marcus and then got in the car to leave with his family.

When the Bentons' car pulled away from the house, Marcus and Marshall were left standing on the porch. "Any plans for today yet?" asked his uncle.

"I thought I would offer to help Gil," he replied.

"That's good. Why don't you plan to come to my study this afternoon after lunch and we'll start going over some things about the business.

"Sounds great, I'm ready!" Marcus answered eagerly.

All the guests were gone now leaving only Emelia, and she was family. With Kate gone for two months, there would be no distractions and Marcus could focus his full attention on learning the business. There wasn't too much left of the morning, but he caught up with Mr. Thompson in the vegetable garden.

"Could you use an extra pair of hands to help with the hoeing this morning?" he offered.

"I sure could. You won't catch me turning down an offer to help. You probably could teach me some things seeing that you have a college degree now."

"Oh, no! I'll always be learning from you," said Marcus. "Books can't teach experience, and you're the master gardener with the knowledge and the experience."

Marcus picked up a hoe, and between the two of them, they were able to finish hoeing the row of beans before lunchtime.

"Sorry, I won't be able to help out after lunch. Uncle Marshall said he was going to start teaching me about the business this afternoon. I'd be glad to help you whenever I can."

"Thank you for your offer," Gil said looking him in the eye. "You're a good worker and a fast learner. With as good a teacher as your uncle is, you'll catch on quickly."

"Thank you for your vote of confidence, I'm eager to learn."

As Marcus entered the study with his uncle, he thought back to that day when "Mr. Jules" had asked to see him. It was here in this same room that he had found out who he was—the great-nephew of the proprietor of Haleub Place. What a long way he had come since that day.

"Sometimes, the best way to teach someone," said his uncle, "is to show them. I've got a business appointment in Westchester this afternoon. I thought I'd take you with me so you can meet Mr. Peeler and observe how we do business. Have a seat." He gestured to Marcus. "There are a few things I'll go over with you now so you'll know what we are talking about when we get there."

Marcus listened intently and took notes as his uncle began to teach him the family business. The world of investments had always been a mystery to him and now he was learning from the ground up. The business courses he'd had in college couldn't teach him what he was about to learn from his uncle. It seemed that no sooner had he settled in his chair ready to learn, then he heard his uncle push back his chair and stand up. A quick glance at the clock let him know that thirty minutes had passed by already.

"That's all you need to know for today. Are you ready to go?"

Startled, Marcus looked up. "I'll be right with you. Let me change my clothes real quick, and I'll be ready in five minutes," he said as he left the study in a hurry.

A smile crept across Marshall's face as he was leaving. With no offspring of his own, this day would never have become reality without Marcus. What a difference he had made in the lives of so may. Wisdom, knowledge, and experience are lost without someone to pass them on to.

A rush of thoughts quickly entered his head as Marcus changed clothes. Right on the heels of graduation and the celebration that accompanied it, he found himself thrust into the unfamiliar realm of the business world. *Am I a man now? When did I cross over from being a boy? Where was that fine line of transition? Was the celebration just for my accomplishments? How do you become a man anyway? Is it something you do yourself, or is it the opinions of others whom you may or may not know?* As he was coming down the hall to meet his uncle, he made a mental note to get back to these thoughts the next time he had a chance.

This afternoon, he had to focus on the business at hand. It was good to see Jake and Julia and their parents, but sometimes it just reminded him of what he didn't have—a home with a mother and a father. He even felt guilty for thinking these thoughts when he was so graciously taken in at Haleub Place and surrounded by so many that loved him. He did have a family—a mother, great-uncle, and grandmother. So why did he feel sometimes like he didn't have a real family? Who knew where he would have ended up if he hadn't come to Haleub Place. He shuddered to think of the possibilities and quickly turned his attention to his uncle Marshall.

"This afternoon should provide some valuable experience," Marshall said as they got in the car to go. "A big part of business is based on relationship, and a good relationship is built on trust. Trust can build wonderful things, just look at what it did for you."

At this, Marcus turned his head just in time to catch the glance his uncle shot his way. His thoughts took him back to those first days and weeks he had spent at Haleub Place. Mr. Thompson had taken great care to build trust with him when he first arrived and that relationship led to gradual trust in others as well.

He was his own example of how to build trust and relationship. He'd never thought about it like that before. Experience is a good teacher if you take the time to stand back and observe what you've learned. Marcus had great love and respect for his uncle, who treated him like a son.

He wished his insides would settle down as he was both excited and nervous about this afternoon. What if he messed up and said something stupid and embarrassed both he and his uncle.

"How did you learn all this, Uncle Marshall? Who taught you?"

"My father took me along with him, just as I am taking you with me."

"Were you ever nervous about it, afraid you might do or say the wrong thing?"

"Yes, I do remember my stomach being tied up in knots on several occasions. In the end it was never as hard as I thought it would be. Most of my fears were based on the unknown, and after I'd been with my father a few times, the fear gave way to anticipation."

"How did you meet all these people in the first place?"

"Building trust, relationship, and word of mouth. When you do something well, people find out about it and tell others. Pretty soon, they are coming to you rather than you seeking them."

In spite of asking questions all the way to Winchester, Marcus was still a bit anxious when they arrived.

The tires crunched on the gravel as they pulled in to park. "You'll do fine. Just be yourself," his uncle encouraged him.

It was a stately old building constructed of rough-hewn gray stone. Two stories high with two windows on each side of the building, upstairs and down. *What a foreboding place*, Marcus thought as he swallowed hard. They quickly climbed the stairs, and Marshall rang the bell. After a moment, the large wooden door opened slowly to reveal a plump little woman with tight blonde curls all over her head.

"Mr. Jules! So good to see you again, sir," she said. "Come in, come in. And who is this you've got with you today?" Her eyes sparkled with excitement.

Marcus was pleasantly surprised by the warmth of their welcome as he heard his uncle say, "This is my nephew, Marcus Williams." He leaned forward, extending his hand, which she clasped between both of hers very graciously.

"We think very highly of your uncle around here. You are very fortunate to have such a fine influence in your life. So nice to meet you, Marcus."

"The pleasure is mine," he heard himself say as his lips parted giving way to a smile. As they were ushered down the hall, Marcus began to relax a bit as he followed his uncle. He was beginning to feel the impact of his uncle's good name being passed on to him. His uncle's name was more valuable than any degree or piece of paper listing his accomplishments. He took a deep breath and squared his shoulders as he stepped into Mr. Peeler's office.

As soon as the Bentons arrived home, Julia and Kate grabbed their suitcases out of the trunk and disappeared into Julia's room. Jake was a bit relieved to see them go as he had listened to their incessant chatter about nothing all the way home. It was good to be home, even if it was just for the summer. He would work on Marcus's request a little later or maybe even wait until tomorrow. It would be several days before the girls would be leaving for their grandparents. Right now, he needed some time to relax. He pulled a book off the shelf in his bedroom and settled down in an easy chair, his feet propped up on the matching footstool. This was his chance to read just for pleasure, not for his studies.

"So, Kate, do you have a boyfriend from school?" Julia asked with a questioning look.

"Not really. I have friends that are boys, but no boyfriend in particular."

"What about Marcus? His whole face lights up when he talks to you, Kate."

"No, it doesn't. We're just friends," Kate replied, brushing off Julia's comment.

"Look, Kate, whether you see it or not, it's pretty obvious that he has feelings for you."

"He's probably met someone at school closer to his age. I'm three years younger than him, Julia."

"Don't you know that if he had met someone at school, he'd have introduced her to the family at graduation? He probably thought you had met someone at school while he was away at college." Julia stretched out on her bed, elbows resting on her mattress to prop up her chin in her cupped hands. She looked straight at Kate sitting cross-legged at the end of the bed. "Face it, Kate, Marcus likes you as more than just a friend."

"Are you sure, Julia? Any assumption on my part could ruin a good friendship really fast."

Both girls were silent for a while, lost in their own thoughts. Suddenly, Julia sat up and looked straight at Kate. "I know...we can get Jake to find out for us. He and Marcus are pretty close. Let's go ask him, I'm sure he is still up."

"You go, Julia. I would feel uncomfortable being present while you were talking about this subject. I'll just wait here until you come back."

Julia winked at Kate as she got up to go down the hall to Jake's room. She could see that his light was still on through the crack under his door so she knocked softly.

"Come in," said her brother.

Julia gently opened the door and closed it behind her as she entered his room.

"What brings you here so late at night?" he asked as he looked up from reading his book. "I thought you'd be talking to Kate."

"Well...we were talking...and we, I mean *I* had a question for you."

"And what might that question be?" he said quizzically.

"Since you know Marcus pretty well, and...maybe he talks to you about important things, and..."

"What are you trying to say, Julia?" he interrupted.

"I'll get right to the point."

"Yes, please do."

"Do you know if Marcus likes Kate? I know they are good friends and they live in the same house, at least when he's home from school, but do you know if he likes her as more than just a friend?"

"Why do you ask? What makes you think that he likes her? Does Kate like him more than just a friend?"

"She says that they are just friends, but I saw the way he looks at her. His whole face lights up when he talks to her. She didn't bring it up, I did. She says she doesn't have a boyfriend from school, and if Marcus had a girlfriend from college, seems like he would have introduced her to the family at graduation."

Jake rolled his eyes at his sister. "I'll see what I can find out. Would Kate want to be more than friends or does she want it to stay like it is?"

"She thought he'd have a girlfriend from college closer to his age since he is a little older than she is."

"But would she be interested in a deeper relationship with Marcus?"

"I think so, but he's been gone off and on for the last four years. He's never said anything to her about it and she sure isn't going to make a move toward him. She's not like that; he would have to make the first move."

"Well, I guess nothing's going to happen for the next two months while you and she are at our grand-parent's house. I'll see what I can find out for you. We haven't had that much time together lately since we've both been at school." He paused, smiled, and continued. "Don't worry; I'll be diplomatic about it."

"Thanks, I knew I could count on you. I'm going to get back with Kate now. Good night," she said as she let herself out.

Jake chuckled to himself. *That was easy. No probing necessary. Nothing like information to come knocking at your door—literally.* And with that thought he put a bookmark in his book and got ready for bed.

Chapter 5

With the excitement and celebration of Marcus's graduation behind her, Lizzy's thoughts turned back to the dream she had had several days ago. *Why would I be thinking about Mitch after all these years? Uncle Marshall was right; I do have things I need to deal with concerning Mitch. I've been carrying a lot of hurt, anger, and bitterness toward him. I made amends with Marcus and Mother years ago. I even made amends with Father at the cemetery, but I never dealt with anything concerning Mitch. That part is stuffed down so deep, that I've forgotten it even existed.* Lizzy fell to her knees right there in her bedroom. With a quivering voice, she began to unload.

"Mitch, I don't know where you are, or even if you are still alive. I choose to forgive you. I'm tired of carrying around this buried pain." Her voice grew stronger as she continued. "I don't know what happened…why you stopped coming home, why you disappeared. I've harbored resentment in my heart against you, and I choose to let it go. I'm sorry for anything that I did that would have caused you to leave. I'm ready to let go of the past and move forward with my life. I take full responsibility for the choices I've made and their consequences, rather than blaming you for everything. I'm sorry things didn't work out for us. Sometimes I wish I knew what happened, and other times I'm glad I don't really know the truth because it might hurt more than not knowing. I wish you could know your son and what a fine man he has become. I'm not sorry for our relationship for it gave me the gift of Marcus. Consider this a farewell that gives me closure to that part of my life."

Lizzy took a deep breath, opened her eyes, and stood up. With all that said, she felt lighter. It was as if a heavy burden she didn't realize she was carrying had been lifted off her. She felt freedom from the stigma of being a single parent. She felt free from being an abandoned wife. She had a new name. Instead of being Lizzy Williams, the abandoned wife, she was Lizzy Williams, the blessed mother of Marcus Williams. What a difference perspective makes.

As she got ready to go to bed, she glanced up in the mirror from brushing her teeth and caught the glimmer of a slight smile on her face. Up to this point, it had all been about Marcus. All that had shifted with his graduation and now he was under Uncle Marshall's wings to learn the business.

Resting her head on her pillow, Lizzy began to allow herself to think back to dreams and desires that she had before she met Mitch. She had always been good at drawing and painting and had one day wished to pursue those interests. The next morning she woke up with a flurry of ideas swirling around in her head. As soon as she got off work that afternoon, she walked a few blocks to the art supply store she had known about but never visited. The little bell at the top of the door jingled as she walked into the store and a saleslady appeared.

"May I help you with something?"

"Yes. I need a sketchbook, some charcoal pencils, and watercolors."

"Right over here," the saleslady said as she led Lizzy to that section of the store.

Lizzy's eyes danced with delight as she fingered the pencils she had not touched for almost twenty years. Her heart leapt with joy as she chose the paper, pencils, and paint. She had not allowed herself any pleasures or extras in so long that she almost felt guilty for making such an extravagant purchase. What was pent up inside her was meant to come out.

Her steps made a lively sound as she walked home to her apartment. She hadn't felt such anticipation since she was a schoolgirl long ago. After setting out her supplies on the kitchen table, she went right to work on her sketchpad. Three hours passed before she looked up and noticed that the light outside was growing dim. The sun had set and it was evening.

"Wow!" she said aloud. "I'd forgotten what a pleasure it was to draw." She made herself stop so she could fix some dinner, and by the time she had cleaned up the kitchen, it was time to go to bed. This time, when she laid her head on her pillow, she felt the joy of accomplishment. What a delight it had been to start sketching again. Perhaps there really was more to life than just getting up, going to work, coming home, going to bed, and doing the same thing all over again the next day.

Marcus found himself fascinated by the seemingly effortless way that his uncle conducted business. It was more of a friendly chat than the harsh haggling he had heard about in his business classes at school. Mr. Peeler asked for his uncle's advice on several matters. They agreed on the terms for the solutions and signed the papers, and that was it. The rest of the time was spent in conversation about a variety of subjects. Several times, he was brought into the conversation, and somehow managed not to make any blunders or say anything stupid that he would regret later.

In parting, Mr. Peeler turned to address him. "Marcus, I can see that you're a lot like your uncle. You have my vote of confidence. You'll do a fine job learning the business, especially since Marshall is the one teaching you. Before you know it, it will all make sense to you."

"Thank you, Mr. Peeler. It was a pleasure meeting you. My uncle has told me some marvelous things about you as well. Thank you for your patience with me while I am in this learning process. If all the clients are as pleasant as you, I'll have no problem at all learning what I need to know."

"Marshall, you've done a fine job with your nephew. Of course, why would I expect anything other than that if you've had a hand in it?"

"You're too kind, Mr. Peeler," replied Marshall.

"No, I know what I'm talking about," returned the gentleman. "You two have a pleasant ride home, and I'll see you next time at your place."

"It's been nice to see you again, as always. Give my regards to Mrs. Peeler and feel free to bring her along with you when you come. Plan on having lunch or dinner with us at Haleub Place, your choice. I'm sure there will be some fresh produce from the garden by then."

"There's no way to refuse an offer like that. Count on us both being there."

With that final remark, everyone stood to their feet, shook hands, and Marshall and Marcus made their way to the door. Once outside, Marcus took a deep breath and let out a sigh of relief.

"That wasn't as difficult as I thought it would be," Marcus remarked to his uncle.

"I told you that you would do fine, didn't I?" Marshall said matter-of-factly. "How about you taking the wheel for the drive home," he said as he handed the keys over to him. "You'll need to learn the way to these places so you can go on your own someday."

Marcus had a dazed look on his face for a few seconds as he let the impact of these last words sink in. Apparently, this learning the business was not going to be as gradual as he thought it would be. His uncle had wasted no time in getting him involved, and he could see now that he would not be holding back in any area.

"Do you have any plans for tomorrow, Marcus?" he said as they got into the car.

"No, my days are open. I told Mr. Thompson I would be glad to help him when I could, but you were going to be teaching me the business."

"How about you coming along when I take Emelia back tomorrow? We'll make some stops on the way home where I can introduce you to some more people."

"Sounds good to me. My time is yours from now on. You're the boss," he said as he pulled out of the parking area.

Marshall turned his face toward his nephew. "That's one thing I'm not. I'm not your boss. I'm your mentor for now. The aim is to partner in this venture, not dictate. That's why I always ask if you have plans and don't assume you don't. There's much more to business than just business. You have to learn how to manage your time, even your personal time. You have to learn how to make decisions and right choices on your own with no one else's prompting. When you build character, you build your business at the same time."

Marcus was silent as he drove on, listening intently to every word his uncle said. His thoughts were racing inside his head. The relief he had just felt a few days earlier in graduating from college was quickly ebbing as he realized that he was now entering another school of sorts. This one, he could see already, would have no graduation ceremony; it would be a lifetime of learning.

As Marshall, Marcus, and Emelia drove off the next morning, Anna and Ellen were settling down into their normal routine when guests were not present. Anna cleaned up the dishes from breakfast, while Ellen straightened and cleaned the room that Emelia had been staying in. It would just be the three of them for lunch. Gil had already been out in the garden for a few hours and would be ready for a break by lunchtime. By noon, all the chores had been done and they decided to eat lunch on the porch to enjoy the gentle breeze of the warm summer day.

"It sure is quiet around here," remarked Ellen, "with everybody gone for the day and the guests all gone as well."

"It is quiet, but I'll be glad for the rest after all that cooking we did for days," added Anna.

Gil winced as he sat down at the table.

"What was that about?" asked his sister.

"What was what about?" he replied, looking up from his plate. He knew better than to try and hide anything from his sister. She had a sharp eye for details and very few things ever went unnoticed by her. Why did she have to notice so soon? He had hoped to slip off to his room after lunch and take a little nap before anyone noticed how tired he was.

"You know I don't miss a thing, especially about you. I saw you wince as you sat down. What's hurting?"

Gil raised his head slowly to meet her steel-blue eyes staring right through him. "I'm just a little tired today from hoeing, Anna. Maybe I've pulled a muscle or something. After a little rest, it should be fine."

"You have been working extra hard lately," added Ellen. "You deserve a little rest now and then."

The three of them ate a leisurely lunch as they sat on the porch and listened to the birds tweet and twitter at the nearby bird feeders.

"Since all our chores are done, how about we all take the afternoon off for a rest," suggested Anna. "I'm sure Mr. Jules won't mind at all. This is supposed to be a place of rest. It wouldn't do for us to be unrested."

They all nodded at each other in agreement and then finished their lunch. Gil headed to his place for a nap, Anna to her room to read for a while, and Ellen chose a book to read in the hammock under the shade trees.

The drive to take Emelia back to Shadowbrook was very pleasant. She praised her grandson for his accomplishments and at the same time assured him that he would have no trouble at all learning the business from his uncle. He was a quick learner and had an excellent teacher.

Marshall parked the car, and he and Marcus each grabbed a bag from the trunk to carry into the house. It was a modest two-story brick home, nestled in an older section of town. The large trees that lined the street revealed the age of this neighborhood as their branches reached out to touch each other, forming an arch down the street.

"Would you two like some lemonade to refresh you after that long drive?" Emelia offered.

"Yes, that would be wonderful," replied Marshall.

"Me too, Grandmother," Marcus chimed in. "Thank you for coming to my graduation. I know it was a lot of extra walking for you and much more excitement than you're used to."

"I wouldn't have missed it for anything, Marcus. I'm very honored to be your grandmother. I wish my sister, Connie, could have been there too. She would have been honored to be your aunt, and Milton, your grandfather, would have loved to have had a grandson. Your mother was only fifteen when her father passed away, just a few years older than you were when I first met you."

Soon she had the lemonade ready and they all sat down at the table to enjoy their refreshing drink.

"Is there anything we can do for you before we head out, Emelia?" Marshall offered.

"If you could set those two suitcases on the bed, it would save me from trying to lift them while they're full."

"Anything else? Now's your chance to get two strong men to help you," he teased as he glanced over at Marcus.

"No. Really, I don't have anything else. The family next door is always checking in on me to see if I need help with anything. They take good care of me."

"Thank you for the lemonade, Emelia," he said as he rose from his chair. "I'll set those bags on the bed for you, and then we'll be off. I promised Marcus that I would introduce him to some more of my business acquaintances today."

"I'll get the bags," said Marcus as he took his last swallow. "That was really good, Grandmother," he said as he set his glass down on the table.

They both hugged her as they said their good-byes and got back into the car. Marshall hadn't been driving long before he turned to enter Northwood Cemetery.

"Why are we going to the cemetery?" Marcus asked gingerly.

"There's someone here I'd like to introduce you to," he said as he parked the car under the big oak tree. "Come on, I'll show you," he continued as they both got out of the car. It was peaceful here as they walked across the grass. There was a gentle breeze and the sounds of birds singing as they flew from tree to tree. "Someday, you're going to have a lot of questions and not know who to ask for the answers. Right here is your grandfather's headstone, Milton Seifert Hopkins. You need to know where he is just so you won't wonder about it."

Marcus was silent as he read the headstone. It seemed that everything was coming at him at once. There were the questions he had about his real father, all the graduation celebration, and directly after that, his entrance into the business world. Now he was in a cemetery faced with another side of his family that he had not given much thought to. What a sobering place.

All of a sudden, he wanted to run and hide somewhere, but how do you run from the thoughts in your head?

Marshall gently broke the silence that seemed to last an eternity, but in reality was only about ten or fifteen minutes. "We can go now," he paused and then continued. "Since we were so close, I thought you needed to know where this place was, even if only for a reference."

Marcus followed him back to the car in silence. He did not know what to say, so remained silent as they drove out of the cemetery.

"I know a good place to stop for lunch over in the next town." Wanting to change the atmosphere a bit, Marshall asked, "Did you ever meet anyone at school that was from Hamilton?"

Marcus shuddered as he tried to refocus and address his uncle's question. "Yes, I think I did meet someone from there, but I didn't know him very well."

"Did your mother ever mention to you where you were born?"

Marcus cocked his head in thought for a moment. "Come to think about it, I don't think she ever did."

Marshall glanced over at his nephew before he continued. "Actually, Hamilton is where I found your birth records. Your mother's marriage license was filed there, which let me know her married name, which led to me finding your birth records." The next time Marshall glanced over at him, he met Marcus's eyes staring at him. "Am I throwing too much at you all at once?"

"No, I need to know these things. Now's as good a time as any." He turned his head to look out the window. "I need to fill in these blanks sooner or later; it might as well be now."

"That's how I was looking at it. I figured the sooner you knew these things, the better off you'd be."

Neither of them spoke during the remainder of the drive to Hamilton. It was a welcome silence for Marcus.

Chapter 6

Gil fell right to sleep as soon as he lay down after lunch. In fact it was already dark when he woke up from his afternoon nap. He got up to fix a bite to eat in his small kitchen and then lay back down again. It was not like him to sleep so much, but he reasoned that he was just tired from all the recent festivities.

It was well past dawn when he awoke the next morning. He glanced at the old clock hanging on the wall and cringed. It was nearly nine o'clock. His usual routine was to be taking a break about this time. He tried to raise up but fell back in his bed again, wincing with pain.

"Ellen, have you seen Gil out anywhere this morning?" Anna questioned. "It's not like him to be late for his morning break."

"No, I sure haven't. I do hope he's all right."

"I'm going over there to check on him," Anna said as she hung up her apron and headed for the back door.

The temperature was quite warm this morning even though there was still a week to go before the official start of summer. The humidity wasn't bad, and there was a gentle breeze blowing. The faint scent of roses was in the air as Anna walked down the short path to Gil's place. She knocked on the door.

"Gil, are you in there?"

A weak voice answered, "Yes, I'm in here."

Anna let herself into her brother's quarters.

"What's going on, Gil? What's hurting? It's not like you to be laid up in bed like this."

"I know, I know." He paused to rest. "I'm so tired, and I hurt all over," he said softly.

"I'm going to get Mr. Jules. He'll know what to do. I'll be right back, Gil."

Anna hurried to the house to find Mr. Jules. She looked all through the downstairs until she came to the closed door of his study. *He must be in there*, she reasoned, *or the door wouldn't be shut*. She quickly knocked on the door.

"Come in," she heard him say.

One look at her face when she opened the door let him know something was wrong. "What's the matter, Anna? You look troubled," he said with great concern.

"It's Gil, sir," she said, still standing in the doorway. "He's still in bed, and he didn't feel well yesterday either."

"That's not like him at all, Anna," he said as he stood up to follow her out of the room.

"No, sir, it isn't," she said as she led the way down the hall.

Mr. Jules reached to open the door for her as they hurried down the path to Gil's place. A quick knock on the door, and they let themselves in to find him still lying in bed.

It was busy at the Benton household that morning as everyone was making the trip to drop the girls off for the summer. Even though Winston's parents only lived three hours away, their visits were limited to two or three times a year. Jake had missed their last visit as he had been away at school. He was eager to see his grandparents again and secretly wished he could stop time for a season and go back to his high school days when he had spent part of his summers with them each year.

Kate was excited to travel to new places and, of course, spend time with Julia. She didn't get to go many places except an occasional visit to her grandparents on her mother's side. She'd never been away for this long, and she was enjoying the time with Julia immensely.

Julia had relayed to her what Jake said about talking to Marcus, and they had agreed to let the subject rest until they heard back from Jake. With all the time Marcus had been away, off and on for the past four years, another two months shouldn't make much difference. Kate had agreed to write to her mother when she got settled in at Julia's grandparents'.

"Is everybody ready to go?" Mr. Benton shouted from the front door.

"Yes, dear, I'm ready," answered his wife from the kitchen. "Just tidying up a bit before we leave."

Jake came around the corner of the hallway. "I'm ready, Dad."

"Well, then, that leaves only the girls," he said as they both suddenly appeared with their suitcases. "Okay, everyone's here. Let's go!"

Lizzy sprang out of bed the next morning. One glance at the clock on her dresser sent her into a flurry of activity. She had overslept but could still make it to work on time if she hurried. *That sure was a good night's sleep. I haven't slept that soundly in a long time.* As she gathered her things together to leave, she glanced over at her sketchbook lying on the table. *I'll get back to that this evening,* she told herself, eager to get her ideas on paper.

The morning sun felt good on her back as she walked briskly down the street to work. Even though her son had lived with her uncle for the past ten years, she still had felt a certain responsibility for him. Somehow, though she didn't completely understand it, his graduation from college was like a release of some sort for her. The challenge of raising a child was complete. He was a working man now, making his own decisions and following his dreams.

What about her own dreams? Did she even have any? She was thankful for her job at the boot factory as it paid the bills, kept a roof over her head, and food on her table, but life was passing by quickly, and she wanted a piece of it before it was gone.

Marcus was glad for the day off tomorrow. He lay in bed thinking about what he would do with it. So much had happened so fast lately that he hadn't had time to catch up with his thoughts. His title for the last four years was suddenly gone. He could no longer say that he was a "student" at Kings College. Some of his teachers had called the students by "Mr." or "Miss" using their last names, but he had never referred to himself as "Mr. Williams".

What was that Uncle Marshall had said? *"You have to learn to make decisions and right choices on your own with no one else's prompting."* He had seemed so sure of himself that night before graduation. Was he ready to become "Mr. Williams," partner of Mr. Jules? Visiting his grandfather's gravesite had been pretty sobering. He had thought a lot about his own father but had never given much thought to his mother's father. Now he was seeing that she had gone from one hurt to another, similar to his own situation. First, she had lost her father, and then she had lost her husband as well. *I guess she didn't have much left to give when it came to me.* In spite of all this hurt, he was still determined to search for his father.

Morning broke with the sun filtering through the curtains in his bedroom. He would seize the day, as he didn't know when his next day off would be. Off to the courthouse in Hamilton, the official search would begin today. He grabbed some fruit and bread for breakfast and left the house before anyone was stirring. This way he could avoid any questions about where he was going. He rode his bike to the station to catch the early train. If anyone wondered where he was, they would see that his bike was gone, and he had left a note saying he was enjoying the day and would be back that evening for dinner.

Winston, Marjorie, and Jake spent the night at the senior Bentons' before heading back the next day. "With the girls settled in for the summer, that should put an end to all this traveling for at least a couple of months," remarked Mr. Benton.

"It should be a lot quieter at the house too." Jake chuckled from the back seat.

"Don't you miss your sister?" asked his mother as she glanced back at him.

"In all honesty, I do, but I'm glad for her and Kate to have this time together with Grandfather and Grandmother. I wouldn't trade those times I spent there over the past summers for anything." He paused as he gazed out the window then continued. "All too soon, those days will be behind them too."

"Son, it's good to have you home again, even if it's only for a few weeks."

"Thanks, Dad. I'm glad to be home too. I miss the time we used to spend together, but you can't turn back the hands of time can you?" Jake shifted in the back seat and gazed out the window again.

He had made great strides in the last ten years and owed much to his parents in all the ways they supported him. Having been born with a birth defect, as a child, he had not been able to walk without leg braces. Through sheer determination, he had relentlessly done leg-strengthening exercises for years and to the doctors amazement was now walking with just a cane. With two more years ahead of him to complete his graduate degree, he had hope that after that he could find a job that would allow him to continue his passion of doing research.

Marcus arrived in Hamilton just as the courthouse opened for the day. Yesterday, when he and his uncle had been there, he had taken note of the office hours and planned his time of arrival accordingly. First, he searched for his own birth record. He found it pretty quickly, given he knew the exact date as well as his mother's full name to verify it. From the birth certificate, he found his father's full name, "Mitchell Troy Williams." Now that he had this information, he wondered what to do next. No one had ever talked about his father so he had nothing to go on.

On a whim, he began his search for his father's birth records. It seemed the logical thing to do and maybe it would give him a clue of what to do next. Not knowing the year he had been born, he started with the same year his mother had been born and worked backwards from there. There were many Williams to search through, but diligence finally paid off. Figuring the math from the birth dates, his father was about three and a half years older than his mother. He glanced at the address and quickly jotted it down as well as his grandparents' full names. He closed the book and returned it to the shelf.

As he was leaving the records room, he glanced at the clock on the wall. It confirmed what his stomach had been telling him. It was time for lunch. He welcomed the fresh air as he stepped outside. The air had been musty and stale in the records room. Across the street was the restaurant where he and his uncle had eaten the day before.

As he walked through the door, one of the waiters recognized him. "Ah. Welcome once again. You liked what you had yesterday and have come back for more. Yes?"

Marcus smiled. "Yes. I did like what I had yesterday, and I am back for more."

"Right this way, sir." The waiter led him to a table right next to the window. "Will you be dining alone, or are you expecting another?"

"No. No others are expected." He sat down as the waiter handed him the menu. "Thank you," Marcus said as he settled himself at the table. A quick glance at the menu and he had made his choice.

The waiter soon returned with his food and he dug in as it had been a long time since breakfast and he had worked up an appetite. As he ate, he pondered what to do next. He knew his father's name now, but where was he to go from here? Reaching in his pants pocket, he pulled out the piece of paper with his grandparents' name and address.

The waiter returned. "Will there be anything else I can get for you today?"

Startled, Marcus looked up at the kind man, then quickly glanced at the paper he held in his hand. "No. No thank you, but could you please tell me how to get to Sycamore Street?"

"Yes, of course," he replied. "Would you like for me to write it down for you?"

"Yes, please." Marcus offered the paper he still held in his hand.

"Ah. You are looking for James and Evelyn Williams?" he read from the paper.

"Yes. Do you know them?" he asked hopefully.

"Not personally, but he runs a repair shop down over on Second Street. That's just a few blocks in that direction," he said as he pointed out the restaurant window.

"Thank you so much." Marcus reached out to shake his hand. "You've been most helpful."

"Oh, it was nothing," he said as he laid the sales ticket face down on the table. "Have a wonderful day, sir, and come back soon."

"Thank you very much." As Marcus rose to go, he left a tip on the table to show his gratitude. He paid his ticket at the counter by the door and then stepped outside into the warmth of the day.

His heart was beating wildly as he walked the few blocks to Second Street. Across the street from where he was standing was the sign that simply said Repair Shop.

Marcus froze as he stared at the storefront window. He hadn't thought this out. *I can't just walk in there and say, "Hello, I'm Marcus Williams, your grandson."* He continued walking right past the shop going a block or two farther just to gain some time. Turning and heading back to the shop, he seized a plan in his mind.

Trembling, he opened the door to the shop. A little bell at the top of the door jingled as he walked in. All around him was a variety of furniture and machines all in a state of disrepair. Each had a tag marking the owner and what was wrong with the item. Soon, an older gentleman appeared from the backroom and eyed his empty hands.

"What can I do for you today young man?"

With the most casual voice he could muster, he replied, "I'm looking for someone who shares the same last name as you and wondered if you might know of him?" Marcus had decided that honesty was the best policy, and he was in fact was looking for someone that shared that description. He took a chance that this might provide him with some valuable information.

"Who is it that you're looking for?" the man answered with no emotion.

"Do you know of a Mitchell Troy Williams?"

"Why do you ask?"

"I have some questions I'd like to ask him."

"Sorry, I haven't seen him in over twenty years. I'm his father."

"Oh," was all Marcus could say at first, his mind racing with what to say next. "Do you have any idea where I might look for him?" he said, scrambling for words.

"He moved out on his own after he graduated from high school. I hear he got married, but we never met his wife." He looked down at the floor for a moment and then right at Marcus. "Can't tell you any more than that."

Marcus froze for an instant. All his hopes of finding his father had suddenly been dashed to the ground. He found his voice and stammered a reply. "Thank you, sir. You've been most helpful. Sorry to trouble you."

The man turned to go to the backroom as Marcus turned to leave the shop.

One look at Gil's ashen face let Mr. Jules know that he was in trouble. "Gil, I think you need to see a doctor," he said gently.

"I'm just a bit tired."

"Now, Gil, you're going to have to trust me on this one. I think you are a bit more than just tired."

Anna stood there quietly wringing her hands, a look of deep concern across her face.

"Maybe you're right," he conceded weakly.

"You don't look like you're in any shape to travel. I'll see if I can send for someone to come out here." He looked at Anna. "Can you stay with him until I get back?"

"Yes, sir, I won't leave his side. You can count on that."

"By the way, have you seen Marcus today?"

"He left a note in the kitchen saying he was enjoying the day and would be back for dinner tonight."

Mr. Jules nodded his head in acknowledgement and headed to the house.

Slowly, Marcus walked the few blocks back to town. In a way, he had discovered a lot, and in another way, he had discovered nothing. Emotionally spent, he decided to head back to Haleub Place early and let this matter rest for a while until he could figure out what to do next.

The ride back went quickly as he just sat, blankly staring out the train window. He welcomed the short bicycle ride from the station as it gave him a chance to collect his thoughts before arriving home.

That's odd, he thought to himself as he noticed the car parked outside. *I didn't think we were expecting any guests today.* He went in the back way to check with Anna and Ellen about who was here.

Nobody was in the kitchen, so he went to knock on Anna's door. No answer. He went further down the hall to knock on Ellen's door. No answer there either. The house was quiet, no voices anywhere. Maybe the guests were resting. He went to his uncle's study. His uncle was nowhere to be found in the house. *Maybe everyone is outside and I just missed them somehow.* As he quickly took inventory of the grounds, he realized Mr. Thompson was not working anywhere outside either. He went to knock on his door, but didn't really expect him to be there. As he neared the door, he heard voices. *So this is where everybody is.*

Chapter 7

As the weekend neared, Lizzy made plans to go to Haleub Place. She was eager to put her talents to work in sketching some of the beauty that abounded there. When Marcus met her at the station, they exchanged hugs and he reached out to carry her small bag.

"Hello, Mother."

"Hello, son. It's good to see you again. Are you taking Gil's place in meeting guests at the station?" she asked cheerily.

"Well, I guess for now, I am."

"What do you mean, for now?"

"I guess you haven't heard yet," he said sullenly. "Mr. Thompson's not doing too well right now." He paused to let that gently sink in. "We've moved him to a guest room on the first floor of the house. That way we can keep a close eye on him."

"What happened? What's going on?" she questioned with deep concern.

"The doctor thinks he may have had a stroke or mild heart attack. It's hard to watch such an active man just lie there in bed." They were both silent for a while as he started up the car to drive home. "He's still in his right mind," he added, "but hasn't got much of an appetite or energy enough to even sit up. He wasn't even interested in fresh strawberries, one of his favorites.

"I'm filling in for now, working on the grounds until Uncle Marshall can find someone to take his place. That's a tall order for anyone. No one could fill his shoes."

Lizzy could sense that her son was taking this hard. He and Gil had a very special relationship, each complementing the other in wisdom and strength. He already had a lot of transition going on right now and this was one more concern added to it. She hoped her visit wouldn't be untimely for anyone.

Uncle Marshall met them as they came into the house. Exchanging hugs, he said, "Lizzy, it's always good to see you."

"Thank you."

"You look radiant! What's different?" he asked with surprise.

"Does it really show?" she asked, unable to hide her feelings.

Marcus turned to look closely at his mother. He had not noticed anything different about her, but they had talked mainly about Mr. Thompson on the way home. Now that he really looked at her, he did notice a twinkle in her eye.

"I've started sketching again, and I couldn't think of a more beautiful place than here to put my talents to work."

"I'm eager to see your sketches, that is, if you brought them with you?" her uncle asked.

"Yes, they're in my sketchbook I brought with me, but first I want to know how Gil is doing. Is he up to having visitors?"

"I'm sure he'd love to see you, Lizzy. He's good for a short visit, but he does tire easily. Anna keeps a sharp eye on him while Ellen tries to help out with Anna's work as much as she can. It's too bad Kate's not here, but she needed the time with a friend, and it's a well-deserved break for her to spend the summer with Julia at her grandparents. We've all shifted our loads a bit to help each other out. That's what family's for."

"Well, I'll be glad to help out in any way that I can while I'm here for the weekend," she offered.

"Talk to Ellen about that, but first, let's go visit Gil," he said as he led the way down the hall to his room.

"You've got a visitor, Gil," Marshall said as he stepped inside the room. "Look who dropped in to see you."

"Lizzy, it's good to see you," he said quietly.

"And you too," she returned.

"Lizzy has started drawing again, and she brought her sketchbook with her."

She reached inside her shoulder bag and pulled out her book. Taking a seat in the chair next to his bed, she slowly showed them one by one and then passed the book to her uncle.

"Those are real fine, Lizzy, real fine." He smiled slightly.

"These are wonderful!" her uncle exclaimed as he studied each one closely. "You've done a wonderful job!"

Lizzy noticed that Gil was blinking his eyes, fighting off sleep, and realized he needed his rest. "I'll stop in again tomorrow. You get some rest now," she said as she got up to leave.

"I'll send Anna your way, Gil," Marshall said as they left the room.

Marcus was sitting in the front room when they returned and Marshall handed him the sketchbook.

"You should see these drawings your mother has here. She's done a wonderful job!"

"I had no idea you could draw like this. You never mentioned it."

"I haven't drawn anything in over twenty years. Just this week, I started sketching again."

That phrase jumped out at him and he froze for an instant. Mr. Williams had said that same thing when he visited his shop earlier in the week. "I haven't seen him in over twenty years."

Marcus hadn't thought much about his father or his visit to Hamilton since he came home that day when the doctor had come to see Mr. Thompson. Marshall and Marcus had lifted him onto the cot that Marcus used to sleep on and then carried him up to the house and eased him off the cot onto the guest bed. Things had taken a turn that day, and nothing had been the same since.

Ellen popped her head in to say, "Dinner's ready," and they all got up to go to the dining room. Marshall kept the conversation going, for which Marcus was grateful. After dinner, he soon excused himself to go to bed early. He was tired physically from working outside all day and just couldn't make conversation anymore. Lizzy and Marshall talked a little while longer and then they both retired early as well.

"I just love your grandparents, Julia," Kate said as she got ready for bed. "I can see why you love coming here so much."

The senior Bentons were a lively couple. He was medium height with a muscular build that portrayed his active lifestyle. Grandfather Benton still had a full head of hair, unlike others his same age. The short dark brown waves went up and down like the waves of the ocean. There was not even a hint of a receding hairline. Grandmother Benton was full of energy as well, always a twinkle in her eye. She was of equal height to her husband and just as trim and active as he was. Her dark gray hair was smoothed back and fastened in a bun at the nape of her neck.

"Jake spent a few summers here when he was in high school. This will be my third summer here," she said as she turned back the covers on the bed. "I'm so glad you're here to spend it with me, Kate!" Her voice trembled with excitement.

The girls shared the double bed in the guestroom upstairs. There was another room upstairs, but it was not really used as a bedroom. Instead, it held a sofa, a few wooden chairs, and a coffee table. There was a door in the corner that opened to a walk-in closet. Numerous boxes lined each side of the space under the eaves. Jake had slept in this room in order for his parents to sleep in the guest room on the ground floor. The grandparents' room was on the ground floor as well. The walls upstairs in both rooms were covered with a yellowed wallpaper of brown tree trunks with green leaves and patches of lavender flowers in clumps of green grass.

"What would you girls like to do today?" Grandmother Benton asked the next morning after Jake and his parents had left to go home. "Your grandfather is out tinkering on something in his workshop. I was about to work on my quilt, that is, unless you two have something else in mind."

"You sew quilts?" Kate asked wide eyed. "Could I see how you do it?"

"Sure, come on in here," she said as she led the girls to the front room. Leaning against the wall behind the door was a quilt rack. In all the excitement upon arriving last night, Kate had not even noticed this rather large apparatus sticking out from behind the door. Stretched out on the frame was a Dresden plate pattern in hues of lavender and light green with strips of patterned yellow cloth between the squares.

"How beautiful!" exclaimed Kate.

"You're almost finished!" Julia said excitedly as she noticed there was only one row of squares that remained to be quilted.

"I'd hoped to be finished before the weather turned warm, but as you can see, it still lacks a bit before I can take it off the frame."

"Maybe Kate and I can help you get it finished, Grandmother," she said wistfully.

"I've never done any quilting before," protested Kate. "I wouldn't know where to start."

"Well, that can be fixed easily, if you're willing," Grandmother said with a determined look in her eye. "Can't it, Kate?" she said as she glanced toward her granddaughter.

"That's how I learned, Kate. Grandmother taught me. It's not hard, really!"

"I'm willing to learn, if you're willing to teach me," she answered eagerly. "When can we start?"

"If you want, we can set it up now." The girls helped Grandmother set up the frame and the quilting lesson began.

Marcus woke up with the sun the next morning. He got dressed and went downstairs to meet the wonderful aroma wafting up from the kitchen. Anna and Ellen were already up and about, having already eaten their breakfast. He soon discovered the source of what had been arousing his appetite. When guests were at Haleub Place, Anna was known for making her famous orange pecan muffins. For a moment, he had forgotten that his mother was here for the weekend, hence the muffins.

Lately, the grounds keeping had given him quite an appetite, even more so than usual. He was grateful for the work outside for it gave him time to reflect on all that had happened in the last few days. There was the business he was learning, the visit to his grandfather's grave, his own trip to Hamilton and what he had found out along with sort of meeting his other grandfather and the situation with Mr. Thompson.

Ellen startled him as she came into the kitchen and found him sitting at the table eating a bowl of fresh strawberries along with the muffins that had been left in a basket on the table. "Good morning, Marcus."

"Looks like I'll be needing to pick some more of these," he said as he popped another of the luscious berries into his mouth. "How's Mr. Thompson this morning?"

"He's doing about the same. It's hard to see such an active man just lying there in bed," she said, shaking her head.

"Well, if anybody wonders where I am, I'll be working in the strawberry patch." He popped the last strawberry into his mouth as he stood up from the table and then went out the back door to the garden shed. He took a deep breath and looked up at the sky. It was a beautiful morning, and he hoped that he could somehow shake this heaviness he felt.

He pulled the baskets out of the shed to collect the strawberries and headed down the path. Mr. Thompson had taught him that it was best to pick berries first thing in the morning when the dew was still on them. That's when they were at their best. He thought back to that first time they had picked and ate them together. It made him smile to remember that first summer when they worked together and lived together in the garden house. Before he knew it, the baskets were filled with the ripe red fruit, and he carried them to the house to set in the kitchen.

"So that's where you've been," said his mother as she eyed what he was carrying. She too had come down for some muffins and then had stayed to help Ellen in the kitchen. Anna was carrying a pile of clean laundry to Gil's room so she could fold it while she sat with her brother. Usually bustling about, it was about as hard for Anna to sit still as it was for Gil. She was devoted to her brother.

Marcus heard male voices in the hallway and wondered who his uncle could be speaking to as he knew there were no guests, besides his mother staying here right now. "I'm just in to drop these off," he said as he placed the full baskets on the table. "I've got some things to take care of in the vegetable garden and then I'll be back in at lunchtime."

"As soon as I finish helping Ellen with a few things, I'll be out with my sketchbook. It's a beautiful day today. Perfect for sketching."

He stood there watching his mother cut up vegetables for lunch. "Yes, it is a beautiful day, Mother. I'm glad you're here. This is what families are supposed to do, help each other."

She caught his eye as she glanced up. "Yes, that is what family is all about, isn't it?"

Marcus stood there a minute longer and then put up his hand to give her a wave and turned to go outside.

Lizzy soon finished what she was doing in the kitchen, grabbed her sketchbook, and headed outside. She settled on a bench in the flower garden and set to work at capturing some of the beauty around her. It was so peaceful out here with the birds singing, the warmth of the sun on her back, and the ever-so-slight breeze. The early spring bulbs had already bloomed and were gone, but there was a new show of color already in bloom, not to mention the subtle fragrance she caught now and again with the breeze. She loved being here.

Marcus was busy hoeing in the garden when he sensed someone nearby. He glanced up and saw his uncle and another gentleman approaching. He straightened up and leaned one arm on the hoe.

"Marcus, I'd like you to meet Mr. Wagner."

"Nice to meet you, sir," he said as he reached out to shake hands with him.

"You too," he replied.

"Mr. Wagner has agreed to come help pick up where Gil left off," his uncle explained. "He'll be staying at Gil's place for now as there's an empty bed there while Gil's up at the house."

Marcus eyed the man as his uncle was talking. He was of dark complexion, with dark brown eyes and hair, probably in his early forties. He had a slight frame but was muscular.

"Would you mind showing him around the place first, and then he can help you with whatever you are working on right now? You know about as much as Gil does about what goes on around here, you've worked with him for so long."

"I'd be glad to show him around, Uncle Marshall. We sure could use another pair of hands around here right now."

"Well, I'll leave you two right now and get back to some things I was working on earlier," his uncle said as he turned to go back to the house.

"This is quite a beautiful place here," remarked Mr. Wagner. "I've heard about it, but never seen it before."

"It sure is," agreed Marcus. "It has been tenderly cared for for years by Mr. Thompson. He knows this place like the back of his hand." Marcus gestured to the area on his left. "As you can see, this is the vegetable garden. Everything's already been planted, I'm just hoeing and mulching wherever it needs it right now." They walked down the path a bit and Marcus pointed out the shrubbery maze as well as the fruit trees beyond it. "All around here is mainly just flowers, bulbs, and bushes, all planted so one thing will be starting to bloom just as others are finishing up. There are benches spaced all about the property for people to just sit and enjoy the beauty."

As they kept walking, Marcus continued, "Over this slight hill and around through this patch of woods there is a clearing with a pond. It's good for fishing," he added. "We can walk out there if you'd like to. I don't mind."

"Why don't we get back to the garden for now," Mr. Wagner suggested. "Now that you've shown me around, I can come back later this evening and take a closer look at things." The two walked back together and Marcus showed him the garden shed where all the tools were kept.

"This is Mr. Thompson's place," he said as he pointed out the building adjoining the shed.

Mr. Wagner grabbed a hoe and looked at Marcus. "Well, let's get after it."

They headed back to the garden and picked up where Marcus had been hoeing earlier. Mr. Wagner eyed the halfway mark and started there so they could each work to the end of their section without being in each other's way.

Now Marcus had something new to add to his list of things to think about. Would this be the new caretaker of the grounds at Haleub Place? Why were there so many changes all at once? He welcomed the familiar rhythm of hoeing and soon was lost in his thoughts again. Before long, they both got to the end of their last rows and finished the hoeing in the garden.

"Are you ready for a cool drink and some lunch, Mr. Wagner?" Marcus asked.

"That sounds wonderful!" he said as he wiped his brow with the back of his hand.

They walked to the back door of the kitchen, and Marcus showed him where to wash up for lunch.

"Have you met anyone else here besides my uncle?"

"No, you two are the only ones I've met so far."

Chapter 8

"Ellen, this is Mr. Wagner. He's here for a while to help us out with the work around the grounds. We've been hoeing in the vegetable garden this morning."

"Nice to meet you, Mr. Wagner. It's usually not so hectic around here, but we're shy three people these days. Mr. Thompson's confined to the bed, his sister, Anna, is tending to him, and my daughter Kate is away for the summer with a friend. Everyone's juggling extra jobs right now, so we're not at our usual pace."

"I understand, Mrs...." He hesitated to know what to call her.

"Silverton," she filled in for him. "Ellen Silverton."

"That's quite all right, Mrs. Silverton, don't let me get in the way. I'm here to help, not hinder."

"Have a seat," she said, kindly, as she gestured to the kitchen table and then turned her attention to the stove.

Marcus excused himself and went to find his mother. He wanted to see what she had sketched this morning. As he walked down the hall, he thought about what Ellen had said, "Three shy." He had almost forgotten about Kate with all the other excitement and changes going on. He wondered if Jake had had a chance to talk with Julia.

He found both his mother and uncle sitting in the front room. "I came to see what you drew this morning. I saw you sitting on one of the benches, but I didn't want to disturb your concentration."

She reached for her book and flipped it open to reveal several birds and some flowers in bloom. He sat down next to her.

"These are really good, Mother. How did you learn to draw like this?"

"I had a few classes in high school, but I think I got my talent from my father. He was always doodling on scraps of paper while he was working."

"How did it go with Mr. Wagner, Marcus?" his uncle inquired.

"He's a good worker. When I was showing him around, he suggested we get back to the vegetable garden and that he would go around later to take a close look at things."

Marshall valued Marcus's observations. "Do you think he'll work out for us? He seems to be pleasant enough. I told him we'd give each other a try for two weeks and then decide from there. That way we can see if we are a good fit for each other."

Marcus agreed, nodding slowly. "That seems fair enough."

Marshall took a deep breath, stood up, and walked over to the front window. He turned back to face Lizzy and Marcus. "Whoever comes to work at Haleub Place, over time, becomes family." He emphasized, "It's very important that we keep that in mind. No one is replacing Gil Thompson; they are only picking up where he left off."

Both Lizzy and Marcus sat quietly as they let his words sink in.

As if on cue, Ellen just then appeared in the doorway, "Lunch is ready if you want to come to the dining room."

While the family ate lunch in the dining room, Ellen fixed a tall glass of lemonade and a plate of food for Mr. Wagner. She set it down on the table in front of him and then turned back to the stove to fix a tray for Anna and Gil.

"Thank you," he said. "It looks and smells delicious!"

"You're quite welcome," she said as she picked up the tray. "I'll be back in a few minutes as soon as I take this down the hall. Go ahead and dig in. Don't wait for me." Her voice trailed off.

"Thank you again, Ellen, for taking care of things in the kitchen for me," Anna said as she took the tray from her. "I know it has been a lot of extra work for you."

"No trouble at all, Anna. I'm glad to help out. You'd do the same for me."

"You're right, I would," she replied. "That's what family is for, helping each other out. Speaking of helping out, did I see someone outside helping Marcus this morning?"

"Yes, a Mr. Wagner is here. He's trying to pick up where you left off, Gil."

"That's good, Ellen. I'm glad Mr. Jules found someone to help out," he replied weakly.

"Marcus has been working on the grounds ever since you went down, Gil," Ellen said, patting his shoulder. "He showed Mr. Wagner around a bit and then both of them went right to work in the vegetable garden. He seems to be a very polite fellow. He's in the kitchen right now eating lunch by himself. I guess I'd better get back there. Enjoy your lunch!" she said as she left the room.

Not long after lunch, Mr. Jules stopped by Gil's room to see how he was doing. From the doorway, he could see the old gentleman was sleeping so motioned to Anna to step out into the hall so that they wouldn't disturb his rest.

"How's he doing, Anna?" he asked with concern.

"He's eating a bit more today, but he's still pretty weak, not able to sit up yet."

"It looks like he'll be needing this room indefinitely then. It will be easier for both of you to have him here, right down the hall from you," he said, nodding his head slowly. "There's a man, Mr. Wagner, that will be staying here for at least two weeks, to help with the grounds. I was wondering if you could get some of Gil's things packed up to bring up here which would make some room for Mr. Wagner to stay there temporarily while he's here."

Reading the concern in her furrowed brow, he added, "I'll stay here and sit with Gil. I've come prepared and brought some papers to go over. Take as long as you need and ask Ellen to help you if you'd like. Have Marcus carry Gil's things up here for you."

"Thank you, Mr. Jules, you think of everything." She stepped back into the room to pick up the lunch tray and then disappeared down the hall.

Lizzy was in the kitchen helping Ellen when Anna brought the tray and set it down on the counter.

Eyeing the dishes, Ellen remarked, "It looks like he ate a bit more today."

"Yes. I thought so too. He's sleeping right now." Anna looked relieved that he was making progress even if it was slight. She washed up the dishes from the tray. It did her good to be in the kitchen again doing familiar tasks.

"Ellen, would you mind helping me get a few of Gil's things together to bring up here to his room? Mr. Jules is sitting with him right now while he's sleeping. He's also asked if we could get the place set for Mr. Wagner to stay there for the next two weeks while he's working here."

"I'd be glad to help, Anna. Lizzy and I are about finished in here anyway."

"Yes, we make a real team," said Lizzy, as she glanced at Ellen. "I'll finish up here, you and Anna go on."

Anna and Ellen stepped out the back door and started down the path.

"There sure are a lot of things changing around here, Ellen. With Gil down and Mr. Wagner here, Kate gone...I guess things can't stay the same forever." She paused as she looked all around the grounds. "It just makes me feel old all of a sudden. I'm so glad that you're here, Ellen," she said with misty eyes.

"I'm blessed to be here, Anna."

As they entered the garden house, Ellen noticed a tear rolling down Anna's cheek. The devoted sister gathered some of her brother's belongings together to take up to the house while she changed the bed linens and washed up the few dishes that were left sitting out on the counter. Gil's place was simple, having only a sitting room with the kitchen along one wall and another room off to the side, which served as a bed-room. On the backside of the building was a lean-to, storage shed–type area where all the garden tools and supplies were kept. Gil lived a simple life and was not much of a collector of things. His real love was the out-doors; it was here where his treasures were planted and thrived. He was a patient man and over the years, many a young man who had thought they were helping Gil with the grounds, had found in the end that he had planted many valuable things in them with his gentle mentoring. Ellen stepped outside to find Marcus and Mr. Wagner. She spotted them working on this side of the shrubbery maze cleaning out the flowerbeds where the early spring bulbs had finished blooming. The warm summer sun felt good on her face as she walked down the path to where they were working. Marcus looked up as he heard footsteps approaching.

"If you two have a minute," she spoke up, "Anna and I have some of Gil's things ready for you to take up to his room. At the same time, we can show Mr. Wagner the place where he'll be staying for the next couple weeks."

"Sure, I'll get him, and we'll be up in a few minutes," replied Marcus. He walked down to where his compan-ion was working.

"Anna and Ellen have the garden house ready if you'd like to take a short break from the garden and see where you'll be staying for the next couple of weeks."

"Sure, let's go," he replied as he stood up and brushed the dirt from his trousers.

"Knock, knock," Marcus said as he opened the door to the garden house. "Anna, this is Mr. Wagner."

"Nice to meet you, sir," she said as she mustered up a smile.

"Anna is Mr. Thompson's sister. I'm going to carry some of his things up to the house for her while Ellen shows you around in here. I'll be back in a few minutes."

Marcus followed Anna to the house and quietly set the things in the hall outside Gil's room as he was still sleeping. He waved to his uncle and then returned to get back to work with Mr. Wagner.

"These two drawers are empty for you to use." Ellen pointed to the chest of drawers standing against the wall in the bedroom. You are welcome to use any of the dishes in these cupboards and the cooking pots are in the cabinet underneath. You are welcome to eat with us in the kitchen or fix your own here. There's always plenty for everyone at the house. The bed has been made and extra linens are in the bottom drawer of that same chest in the bedroom." She paused and surveyed the room. "Is there anything I've left out?" she asked.

"No, no. You've covered everything. Thank you so much for this place to stay while I'm here. I'm much obliged, Mrs. Silverton," he said earnestly.

"Well, then, I guess you're all set. I'll get back to the house. You can move your things in anytime," she said as started for the door.

Mr. Wagner quickly reached for the door and opened it for Ellen.

"Thank you."

"You're very welcome, Mrs. Silverton," he said as he closed the door behind him. He hesitated for a moment and then went down the path to finish up in the flowerbeds.

Marcus passed Ellen coming into the house as he was going out. He joined Mr. Wagner and together they finished the flowerbeds.

"What next?" he said to Marcus as they stood to rest for a minute.

"Let's see…" Marcus said as he stroked his chin with his fingers and took inventory of the grounds in his mind. All the seeds have been planted in the vegetable garden, and the flowerbeds are finished. The next place that needs attention is the flowerbeds in the front of the house. Gil had a way of tending to each spot before it looked like it needed attention. He made it look effortless, but he was always busy doing something somewhere."

"This is a very well cared-for place," observed Mr. Wagner. "It will be a joy to work here," he said as he gazed around the grounds.

As the two carried their tools around front, Marcus noticed his mother sitting on the front porch with her sketchbook open. She looked up and waved as they stopped in front of her.

"Mr. Wagner, I'd like you to meet my mother, Lizzy Williams."

"It's nice to meet you, Mrs. Williams," he said as he nodded his head politely.

"And you, also." She replied.

"We were going to work out here in these flowerbeds, but we can go somewhere else, if it will disturb you."

"No, no. You won't disturb me at all. I've got quite a few sketches done already, and it won't bother me a bit if you're working out here. Please, go right ahead."

Marcus and Mr. Wagner got right to work weeding and cleaning up the flowerbeds. Lizzy sat and watched them for a while then turned the page and began a new sketch. This one seemed to take longer than the others, but she kept at it until it was finished. She gently closed her book and went inside to see if she could help Ellen with anything in the kitchen. The men worked out front until the job was done.

Marcus surveyed the flowerbeds as he wiped his brow with the back of his hand. "We've done a lot today. Why don't you go get settled in the garden house? Dinner should be ready in about half an hour. Thanks for all your help today. We won't be working tomorrow so you can stroll around the grounds at your leisure and look at things more closely then."

They carried their tools back to the shed and then parted, Marcus to the house and Mr. Wagner to get his things from the car. As Marcus walked through the kitchen, he noticed his mother helping Ellen get dinner ready.

"Something smells awfully good in here, and I'm ravenous!"

"Not too much longer," his mother said as she glanced at him over her shoulder. "How did it go out front?"

"The beds out front are finished! Mr. Wagner is a good worker and he really knows what he's doing!" He breathed in the wonderful aroma of dinner. "I can't stand it in here much longer. I'm going to get cleaned up so I'll be ready when you are." And with that said, he disappeared down the hall.

"You have a fine son, Miss Lizzy," Ellen said smiling. "A hard worker with a pleasant disposition, what a wonderful combination.

"He had a great teacher in Gil. He's taken it hard since Gil's been down." She looked up from the pot she was stirring on the stove. "Those two have a very special relationship."

"Yes, they sure do," Ellen said as she slid a tray of biscuits into the oven. "I'm going back to go check on the table in the dining room to make sure everything's set. Dinner should be ready as soon as the biscuits are done."

Lizzy was grateful to have been of some help this visit. Everyone at Haleub Place had been so good to her and her son that it felt good to be able to give something back for a change. Seeing, smelling, and helping to prepare the food had stirred her appetite as well. She never cooked like this for herself and she thoroughly enjoyed the meals here on her visits.

Ellen was back soon, and they started filling the serving dishes to take to the table. The biscuits were ready, a nice golden brown, and smelled delicious.

"I'll take this basket of biscuits out to the table, Ellen, while you take the tray for Gil and Anna.

"Thank you, Lizzy. If Mr. Wagner shows up while I'm gone, tell him I'll be right back."

As if on cue, Mr. Wagner showed up just as Ellen disappeared down the hall.

"Ellen said to tell you that she'd be right back. I'm going to take these to the dining room. Enjoy your dinner." And off she went through the door to the dining room. "I've got hot biscuits," she said as she set the basket down on the table and took her seat.

"I can't wait to taste them," Marcus said as he reached in the basket to get some and then passed it to his uncle. "Mmmm, these are so good," he said as he quickly took a bite before they even reached his plate.

Chapter 9

Things had settled down quite a bit since Mr. Wagner had come to Haleub Place. Marcus had worked with him a few days until he was familiar with the grounds and everything that needed to be done. It was obvious that he knew what he was doing and Marshall had felt confident enough to release him to work without Marcus. He still had another week to go in the two-week trial period, and they could make further arrangements when that was completed.

There was slight improvement in Gil's appetite, but he was still too weak to sit up in bed. The doctor said he'd had a stroke and it would be a matter of time before he gained his strength back. Someone his age might not regain at a hundred percent. This was grim news to everyone, especially his sister.

Anna was devoted to her older brother, who was fast approaching his eighty-sixth birthday. She stayed with him day and night as there were two twin beds in the room. She was not far behind him in years herself, and Mr. Jules had insisted there be a bed brought in for Anna so she would be able to rest.

No guests were expected until the end of next week, giving Marshall another opportunity to take his nephew with him to a business appointment. He had been very distracted by the events of the last few weeks concerning Gil and working with Mr. Wagner.

Marshall handed the keys to Marcus as they walked across the porch. "Would you mind driving?"

"No, not at all. Just tell me where we're going and how to get there."

"We're going to see a Mr. Horner in Chesterfield, about two hours west of here. He's expecting us around eleven o'clock, and we'll be having lunch with him as well. This will be a good change of scenery for you to get your mind off Gil."

They both got in the car, and Marcus pulled out of the parking area. As they drove away from the house, Marshall turned his head to look out the window.

"You know, this place will outlive all of us, Marcus. My father had great foresight in the layout of the grounds as well as the house and the outbuildings."

Marcus didn't know what to say in reply, so he just kept silent. His uncle's comments didn't really require a response, and anything he could think of to say right now would sound forced.

Turning his head toward Marcus, Marshall continued. "What do you think about Mr. Wagner? Remember what I said to you and your mother the other day? Whoever comes to work at Haleub Place over time becomes family. Do you think that you could, over time, come to consider him as family?"

Marcus took a moment before he answered. "Yes, I think I could. He's a very pleasant fellow and knows what he's doing." He glanced quickly at his uncle as he drove on. "How is it that someone with his ability is not already working somewhere?"

"Good question, Marcus. When I was asking about his experience, he told me that until recently, he had been working for a family as their groundskeeper. The husband had passed away, and his elderly wife, not wanting to live there alone, had sold the place and moved in with one of her children. His situation works well with our need. I thought I would talk it over with you first before saying anything to him. Perhaps we would be a good fit for each other.

There was a letter waiting for Marcus when he and Marshall returned home later that afternoon. He picked up the letter to read the postmark—Whispering Hills. This must be the letter he was expecting from Jake to let him know about Kate.

"I'm going upstairs to my room for a bit until dinner's ready," he said to his uncle as he headed for the stairs. He was eager to read this letter in the privacy of his own room.

Dear Marcus,

Sorry it's taken so long to write to you, time got away from me. My job of getting information for you was made quite easy by Julia. Before the girls went to stay at my grandparents, she knocked on my door to ask me some questions. She wanted to know if I could find out for her if you liked Kate as more than a friend. She said it was pretty obvious to her and questioned Kate about it. Kate said she figured you probably had a girlfriend from college that was close in age to you. Julia assured her that if you had had a girlfriend at school, you would have introduced her to everyone at graduation.

Bottom line is that you would have to be the one to make the first move and see where it goes from there. She doesn't have a boyfriend from school, so there's no interference. I think you two would make a great couple. You're already friends and respect each other; that's a huge part of a relationship.

So, that's the news from Whispering Hills, and on another note…

Jake wrote more, but that was all he said about Kate. He wondered if Kate knew about Mr. Thompson and then reasoned that her mother had probably written to her about it. Marcus hoped things at Haleub Place would be a bit calmer by the time Kate got back. It looked like things were going to work out with Mr. Wagner and that would take a big load off everybody.

By the end of the week, Marcus had a plan. He got up early Saturday morning to catch the train to Griffin. Never having been to his mother's apartment, he thought he would meet her on her ground. It would feel very awkward to talk about his father at Haleub Place. He did not want anybody there to think he was ungrateful for anything.

It was a warm late June morning as he got off the train and walked the short distance to his mother's apartment, It was not a large building, only two stories high with four apartments. The gray stone building had a large window on every side with a small lawn in front and back. A narrow sidewalk branched off the main sidewalk measuring about fifteen feet from the road.

Music could be heard softly playing from the open window upstairs on the right. The mailboxes in the hallway downstairs revealed this apartment as his mother's. At least he knew that she was already awake. He climbed the stairs and knocked on the door. Slowly the door opened.

"Marcus, what a pleasant surprise! Come in, come in. What brings you here on your day off?"

"I realized that I had never come to see you before and thought I would drop in for a visit. I didn't think you'd mind."

"No, I'm glad you came. Sit down and make yourself at home," she said as she gestured to the small brown couch. The room was sparsely furnished with a small table and two chairs against one wall. The large window he had seen from the street was in the middle of the front wall, and a small kitchen was against the wall that backed up to the stairway. Off to one side was a small bathroom and a door to what he assumed was a bedroom.

"When did you draw that?" he said, pointing to a sketch of himself that was tacked to the wall above the table.

"The other day when you and Mr. Wagner were working out front in the flowerbeds, it was a perfect opportunity without you even knowing what I was doing."

"It's really good, Mother. You are very talented."

"Thank you, Marcus. I didn't realize how much I enjoyed doing it." She picked up a bowl of fruit from the kitchen counter and offered it to him.

"Thanks," he said as he helped himself to some cherries.

"So what brings you here to the fair city of Griffin today?"

"Well, I've had some things on my mind that I'd like to ask you about."

Her stomach began to turn a bit as she braced herself for the questions she had known he would most likely ask someday. She sat down on the other end of the couch. Nodding her head toward him, she heard herself say, "Sure, what's on your mind."

Almost as nervous as she was, he glanced at the floor and then back at his mother. "Do you know anything about my father's family?"

"No, he never introduced me to his parents and said he didn't have any brothers or sisters."

"Do you ever wonder about his family?"

"No. He didn't have much of a relationship with his parents, nor did I with my own mother. He was living on his own when I met him and neither of us had any regard for our parents at that time in our lives."

"Uncle Marshall and I went to Hamilton one day for lunch after we dropped off Grandmother at Shadowbrook. He told me I was born in Hamilton."

Lizzy nodded her head. She was beginning to loosen up at the chance to finally talk openly with her son about her past.

"I've been wondering about my father for some time now, as I really don't know anything about him other than he just left one day and never came back. I don't even know what he looks like."

"He was tall, six feet four, with light sandy brown hair and brown eyes. He was strong and handsome, easygoing and friendly. Everybody liked him." Lizzy drew her feet up under her and paused for a minute. "I thought he loved me, as I truly loved him. I honestly don't know what happened that made him leave."

"I went back to Hamilton by myself the next day, the day Mr. Thompson had a stroke. I looked up my birth certificate to give me his full name, and then I looked up his birth certificate, which gave me his parents name and old address. On the way to checking out their address to see if I could find any trace of them, I stumbled on his place of business. When I stopped by his shop, I asked if they by any chance knew of a Mitchell Troy Williams. He told me he hadn't seen him in over twenty years and that he was Mitchell's father."

Marcus paused for a minute and then continued. "I didn't know what else to say at that point so I thanked him and left the store. Without knowing any details from you, I didn't want to just blurt out, 'Hey, I'm your grandson.' He said he had heard about his son's marriage, but it's my understanding that my father doesn't even know that I exist."

Stunned, Lizzy sat there for a while without saying anything. "I've never met your father's parents. I really don't know what they know."

As she sat there lost in her own thoughts, Marcus reached for another handful of cherries. This whole conversation had gone more smoothly than he had anticipated and his nervousness about this meeting had begun to dissipate.

Lizzy got up to get a drink of water and offered her son a drink as well. Walking back to the couch to sit down, she handed a matching glass to her son. After taking a long drink, she looked Marcus squarely in the eyes.

"If Mitch's parents are anything like my mother, they would probably be thrilled to know that they had a grandson. Perhaps you could write a letter to them and send it to the business address. If they answer your letter, it would be a good way to sense how they feel about you, rather than just introducing yourself without any warning."

"That's a good idea, Mother. I think I'll do just that." He hesitated a minute. "Do you think Uncle Marshall would be offended by me trying to find out about my father? I don't want him to think that I'm ungrateful for all he's done and is still doing."

"I think you'll find him very understanding and maybe even helpful in your search. He was pretty good at finding me...and uncovering who you were, Marcus. I'm glad you came today and that we had this chance to talk. I wish things hadn't been so hard for both of us over the years, but I think it has made us stronger for having gone through those hard times.

"I know that I've said this before, but I just want you to know how much I appreciate you giving me another chance to try and be a better mother to you." She shifted in her seat and then asked, "How are you liking learning the business so far?"

"It's very interesting, especially meeting the clients. I'm learning a lot about people as well as business and making a lot of contacts. Uncle Marshall is an amazing businessman. It all seems so effortless to him."

"I agree—he is a pretty amazing man."

Kate was a fast learner, and before the end of the week, she had helped Julia and her grandmother to get the quilt finished. As the two girls admired the finished work, Mrs. Benton put away the pins, needles, and thread. They leaned the empty frame against the wall behind the door.

"Kate, I want you to have the quilt to take home with you at the end of your visit."

"Oh, no, I couldn't, Mrs. Benton," Kate protested. "It's too beautiful, and you've put so much work into it."

"I have plenty of quilts around the house, and Julia already has one from me. I insist—this one is yours."

"Thank you so much! It will be a memento of the summer I spent here. I'll always remember you and Julia when I look at it."

Julia was beaming, grateful for her grandmother's generosity and touched by Kate's thankfulness.

"What shall we do next?" asked Julia. "Do you have any more unfinished projects Kate and I could work on?"

"Not right at the moment, but your grandfather is working on some birdhouses out in his workshop. I've got to get some laundry done this afternoon. Maybe you two could hang it on the clothesline for me."

"Sure, we'd be glad to," offered Julia. "Let's go see what grandfather's doing with the birdhouses," she said to Kate. As the girls walked outside to the shop, Mrs. Benton went to get the laundry started.

Mr. Benton looked up as he heard the door open and greeted the girls with a big smile. "Come on in, girls. Welcome to my workshop, Kate."

Kate's eyes were drawn to the three wooden birdhouses on the table. All four sides had been attached to the bottom piece and two were lacking a roof. He had been hammering the roof on to one of the birdhouses as the girls came in.

"Those birdhouses look like the ones at Haleub Place," Kate said.

"That's because grandfather made the ones at Haleub Place," Julia answered. "Mother insisted that we give some to Mr. Jules as a present."

"I like to make things, and as you'll soon find out, we have quite a few birdhouses already at our place, so I've been giving them away so others can enjoy them."

"Do you mind if we watch you for a while?"

"Not at all. You and Kate can pull up those stools over there," he said as he pointed to the far end of the shop.

They watched as he finished the roof on the first one and then handed it over to them as he started on the next one. Two shingles went on each side of the roof. There was a hole cut out on one side with a peg sticking out below it to act as a perch. It wasn't long before all three birdhouses were complete.

Mr. Benton glanced at the clock. "It's almost lunchtime," he said. "Let's go see what Grandmother's got cooking."

As they walked in the back door, Grandmother met them at the door with a basket of clean laundry. "There's just enough time to get this on the line before lunch, if you don't mind girls?" she said.

"We don't mind at all," Julia said as she glanced at Kate, "do we?"

"No, with both of us out there, it should go really fast," answered Kate.

"I'm glad Kate came with Julia this summer," Hazel said to her husband as the screen door slapped shut in the kitchen. "They're good for each other, and so helpful."

"They are a joy to watch," he agreed as he washed his hands at the sink. As he sat at the table waiting for lunch to be ready, he sifted through the mail that had been delivered that morning. "Here's a letter addressed to Kate from Haleub Place. I'll set it at her place so when she sits down she'll see it."

Chapter 10

Mr. Wagner was sitting in Mr. Jules's study as the two weeks they had agreed on was up.

"Now that you've had a chance to work the grounds for a while here at Haleub Place, how would you feel about continuing?" questioned Marshall.

"I've enjoyed it here very much. It's a well cared-for place, and I would like very much to continue here if given the opportunity."

"It would be best for Mr. Thompson to stay up here at the house, so if you don't mind living in the garden house, we'll move the rest of his things up here and that will give you a little more space."

"How is Mr. Thompson doing?" he inquired, concerned.

"He's gaining his strength back, little by little. He's able to sit up in bed now and his appetite is perking up a bit."

"Do you have any family, Mr. Wagner?"

"I have a brother and his family who live over in Hamilton. That's who I've been staying with since the place where I used to work sold."

"A fellow as handsome as you, not married?" Mr. Jules said as he cocked his head to one side.

"I was married at one time. My wife and infant daughter died within a week of each other. She was only one week old. They both died of pneumonia. It's been fifteen years that they've been gone now."

"I'm sorry to hear that. It's hard to lose someone you love." Mr. Jules sighed, then stood and held out his hand. "We're glad to have you here with us, Walter," he said as they shook hands in agreement. "Feel free to take the next couple days off if you need to go gather your things from your brother's. We'll get Mr. Thompson's things moved out before you get back. Check with Anna before you go to see what furnishings you need so we don't move anything out that you need."

"Thank you, sir. Thank you very much! I'm looking forward to coming here to stay. It will be a pleasure working here." He stood, holding his cap in one hand, and headed down the hall to find Anna.

Marcus sat at the desk in his room and stared blankly out the window. Trying to compose this letter was not as easy as he'd thought it would be. So far, all he had written was "Dear Mr. And Mrs. Williams," but then he struck through that and wrote, "Dear James and Evelyn Williams." This was going to be one of those letters that needed a rough draft before the actual letter would be copied over and sent. He tried again.

> *Perhaps you may remember me. Several weeks ago, a young man stopped by your shop looking for Mitchell Troy Williams. You told me that you were his father and that you hadn't seen him in over*

twenty years. Not knowing what to say next, I thanked you and left the store.

A couple weeks passed before I had the opportunity to ask my mother a few questions. Her name is Lizzy Williams, and she said she had never met either of you. She and Mitch had been married only a few months when he came home one night, took his clothes, and left with no explanation. That was the last time she saw him. A few weeks later, she found out she was pregnant with me. The next ten years were pretty difficult for us both, but for the last ten years I've been living with my great-uncle. My mother and I have a pretty good relationship with each other now.

I know this news may come to you as a shock, and I apologize for that. Lately, I've been very curious to find out anything I can about my father. I looked up my birth certificate, then my father's as well, and that is where I learned your names and address. On my way to visit you, I was referred to your repair shop. Just showing up and saying 'Hi, I'm your grandson,' didn't seem right, which is why I am sending this letter to you.

Respectfully,

Marcus Williams

P.S. I am including my return address if you care to make further contact. If not, I understand.

He'd finally gotten his thoughts down on paper. Now he would let it rest for a day or two before he sent it.

Guests were expected this afternoon, and he had promised Anna that he would help move the rest of Mr.

Thompson's things to the house. She and Ellen were busy in the kitchen preparing for dinner. Since Gil was doing a bit better, she had left a small bell for him to ring if he needed help with anything. She checked on him frequently to ease her mind.

Mr. Jules was trying to locate a wheelchair for Gil so they could let him sit on the front porch and get some fresh air now and then. With Mr. Wagner moving in to stay, things should settle down in regard to the upkeep of the grounds. Things had been nonstop since graduation and half the summer was gone already.

Marcus laid an old piece of cloth over the wheelbarrow and began to load it with the things that Anna had set out to be moved. He thought back to the day when he had moved from this place to the room he had now on the second floor. Things don't stay the same for long. Life keeps moving forward, old things pass away and new things break forth.

As he rolled the rest of Mr. Thompson's things toward the house, he thought about the minimal amount of material accumulation that lay before him versus the wealth of relationships and physical planting and tending to of the grounds that surrounded him. He paused at the back door before carrying in the contents of the wheelbarrow and took a few moments to survey everything around him. One day, he would be responsible for all this. The choices and decisions he made now would not only affect his future, but also touch the lives of countless others.

He leaned over and began loading one arm full of things to carry in. He rested in the fact that, in time, his uncle would teach him all that he needed to know.

"Where would you like for me to put these things, Anna?" he said, as he entered the kitchen.

"I've cleaned out a space to the left of the dresser. You can lay them on top of the small rug there on the floor. Thank you so much for moving all that for us," she added.

"Glad to have been of help. I've just got a few more things to bring in and then it's done," he said as he started down the hall. "Knock, knock," he said with a smile as he stood in the doorway.

"Come in, Marcus. It's good to see you again." He motioned to the empty spot by the dresser. "Anna's got a spot cleared out over there. Thanks for bringing my things."

"Now, we both have moved up to the 'big house,'" he said as he set the load down.

"Sometimes we have to move on to make room for somebody else."

"Have you met Mr. Wagner yet?"

"No, but I've heard good things about him."

"You'd like him. I'm sure he'd like to talk to you when you're up to it. He knows what he's doing and is a good worker too, very pleasant fellow." Heading for the door, Marcus turned to say, "I'll be back in a minute with the rest of your things."

He gathered the remaining items from the wheelbarrow and took them to Mr. Thompson's room. "Are you up to talking for a few minutes, or would you rather rest? I can come back later if you're getting tired."

"No, no, have a seat." He gestured to Marcus. "You've been so busy doing my job that I haven't got to see you much." He looked intently at Marcus. "So you think Mr.

Wagner will work out? You've worked with him, and I value your opinion."

"Yes, I do. His misfortune in being let go when his former employer's property sold has worked to our benefit. We needed each other at the same time." He changed the subject. "So how are you feeling these days?"

"I can't complain; I'm still ticking," he said with a twinkle in his eye. "I guess it was just time to retire. Seems that since Mr. Wagner needed a job, this gave me a chance to bow out gracefully."

They sat and talked for a while until Marcus noticed that Gil's eyes were beginning to droop. "I've enjoyed talking with you, and I'll stop by more often now that you're feeling better." He touched him on the arm as he stood up to go. "You get some rest now."

"Thanks for bringing my things and sitting with me. Please come back soon."

"I will. You can count on that."

As Marcus walked back through the kitchen, he glanced at Anna and Ellen. "Anything else I can help either of you with today?"

"Not that I can think of," said Anna, "but our guests should be arriving within the hour. Mr. Reed is here on business and is bringing his wife and two children. I expect your uncle will want to introduce you."

"Well, I guess I'd better get this wheelbarrow put away and get cleaned up for our guests."

Anna was humming to herself as she and Ellen were preparing dinner. Marcus had learned long ago that when he heard her humming it meant all was well. He whispered to Ellen as he walked by and pointed toward Anna standing at the stove with her back toward him, "She's humming again."

They both smiled as he headed toward the back door. The only one missing now was Kate, and it would be several weeks before she was back.

Kate saw the letter at her place when she sat down for lunch. Not wanting to read it at the table, she picked it up and slid it into her pocket.

"What would you girls like to do this afternoon?" asked Mrs. Benton. The quilt's finished, the laundry's done, and Grandfather says the birdhouses are finished too."

"Can we go into town for some ice cream?" Julia asked, hopefully.

"That's a great idea," said Mr. Benton. "I need to pick up a few things for my next project."

"I could use a few more things from the grocery store," his wife added.

"You'll love their ice cream, Kate," Julia said excitedly.

"I'm glad you two came to visit this summer," Mrs. Benton said as she passed the steaming bowl of chicken and dumplings to Kate. "It would have been awfully quiet around here without you here."

"Kate, have you ever played dominoes?" asked Julia's grandfather.

"No, I never have," she answered politely.

"Would you like to learn," he said expectantly.

"Sure," she said as she passed the bowl to Julia, who was chuckling by now.

"Kate, you've been caught in Grandfather's trap."

"What do you mean?" she asked quizzically.

"You'll see." Mrs. Benton nodded as they all sat there grinning at her.

Kate knew by the look on their faces that they weren't going to let the secret out. Whatever it was, it couldn't be too bad because everyone seemed to be very amused.

As soon as lunch was over and the kitchen cleaned up, everyone got in the car to go to town. The Bentons lived in a rural area about thirty minutes from the center of town. They usually waited until they had several errands to run rather than driving back and forth a lot. This was their first time to town since Julia and Kate had come to visit.

"Ice cream first or last?" asked Julia's grandfather, looking in the rearview mirror at the girls in the back seat. He was approaching the town square and needed to know where to park.

"Let's do ice cream first," Julia offered. "That way Grandmother's groceries won't have to sit in a hot car."

"Good thinking. I'll park at the grocery store. That way when we finish eating ice cream, everyone can do their errands and meet back at the grocery store." He winked at Julia. "I'm sure you and Kate can find some store to go into while your grandmother and I are picking up the things on our lists."

"That sounds good to me," Julia said as they pulled into a parking place.

The four of them walked together the half block to Belinda's Diner. It was really a restaurant but was known for its ice cream as well. A bell at the top of the door jingled when Mr. Benton opened it to let the ladies in first. Several seats were open at the counter, so they sat there rather than a booth. In Julia's mind, being able to sit on a swivel seat was part of the experience of getting ice cream. The menus were nestled between the salt and pepper shakers and the napkin holders on the counter. Kate was the only one that picked up a menu as the others already knew what they were going to order.

Julia leaned close to Kate, "My favorite is butter pecan."

There were only seven flavors listed in the dessert section: vanilla, chocolate, strawberry, neapolitan, butter pecan, peppermint, and spumoni.

"What can I get for you today?" the waitress asked cheerily.

Mr. Benton pointed to the girls as the place to start.

"I'll have butter pecan," spoke up Julia.

Poised with her pencil ready to write, the waitress looked at Kate.

"I'll have spumoni, please."

Next was Mrs. Benton, "I'll have neapolitan, thank you."

"And I'll have chocolate as usual," said Mr. Benton.

"It'll just be a few minutes," said the waitress as she turned to go fill their orders.

"Is that you, Archie?" said a man's voice from behind them.

Mr. Benton turned on his chair in the direction of the voice.

"I thought I recognized your voice, but I couldn't place the two young ladies sitting here with you and your wife."

"Well, hello, Charlie. It's good to see you." He pointed to his right. "These two young ladies are Julia and Kate. Julia's our granddaughter and Kate is a friend of hers."

"Hello, Charlie," Hazel said as she turned to greet the gentleman sitting a couple booths away from them.

"Nice to meet you," said Julia and Kate in unison.

"How's your wife, Ann, doing?" questioned Archie.

"She should be coming home at the end of the week. The doctors say that in time, she should be able to go from a walker to a cane and then back on her own two feet."

"That's good news," said Archie.

"For both of you," added Hazel. "We'll come by to visit when she get's home."

The waitress brought their orders, and they turned their attention to the dessert sitting in front of them. Each bowl was filled with a generous scoop of ice cream and two large shortbread cookies tucked in on either side.

"Mmm, this is so good. Thank you," Julia said leaning toward her grandparents.

"Yes, it is delicious. Thank you very much." echoed Kate.

"Good idea you had, Julia," said her grandmother, savoring a bite of cookie with her ice cream.

"Yes, I agree," said her grandfather.

When every bowl was empty, and the bill paid, they slid off their stools to leave the diner. Mr. and Mrs. Benton waved good-bye to Charlie with a promise to stop by when Ann got home.

"Let's all meet at the car in about an hour," said Julia's grandfather. "That should give everybody time to look around as well as get our errands done."

They split up in different directions, Mr. Benton to the hardware store, Mrs. Benton to the grocery store and Julia and Kate went to the new gift store that had opened since Julia's last visit to town. They were not shopping to buy anything in particular, just looking to pass the time.

"That was really nice of your grandparents to take us all to the diner. You are really blessed to have such a wonderful family, Julia."

"What are your grandparents like, Kate? You never talk much about them."

"I only see my mother's parents on holidays and my father's parents live too far away to visit. The last time I saw them was at my father's funeral."

"I'm sorry that you don't get to see them more often. You must miss them. I'm glad that you could come with me for the summer. It makes my visit even more special than if I had come by myself."

"I'm glad I got to come. This is a very special time for me too."

Time passed quickly as the girls looked through several shops on the square. They all met back at the car at the agreed time and headed home. As Kate sat in the back seat listening to Julian and her grandparents chatting away, she suddenly remembered the letter that she had slipped into her pocket at lunch. She pulled it out and opened it.

Dear Kate,

Hope you are having a wonderful time with Julia and her grandparents. I miss you and your smiling face. It's been very busy around here, but we're managing somehow...

I hate to have to tell you this in a letter, but it's
better for you to prepare yourself than to come home
and be totally shocked by all the changes...

She read on intently, completely oblivious to the conversation in the car.

Mr. Thompson has had a stroke and is in a room
down the hall... A Mr. Wagner is living in the garden house now...

By now, her eyes were so misty that she could no longer read the letter so she folded it up and turned her gaze out the window. Julia noticed Kate's hand brushing away a tear from her cheek and decided to wait until they got to the house before she asked about the letter. She kept the conversation going with her grandparents to cover for Kate who she could sense was trying to keep her composure.

Chapter 11

Lizzy was glad that Marcus had taken it upon himself to seek out information concerning his father. She had been too hurt to do anything on her own. She knew now that her pain had immobilized her from moving forward in her life. Up until recently, she had thought her mending was done. After working through her relationships with her son and her mother and making peace with her deceased father, Lizzy was back with her family.

Her recent dream had brought things up that she thought were buried and over. Since she had let forgiveness into her life, she was really learning how to live again. If Marcus had asked her about his father even just a month ago, she would have had only negative things to say about him. Now, she could appreciate and understand his curiosity without feeling threatened in any way.

The fact that Mitch's parents hadn't seen him in over twenty years made her appreciate their probable state of confusion and hurt concerning their son. She and Marcus most likely weren't the only ones hurting.

If Marcus followed through and wrote the letter to his grandparents, perhaps that would open up an opportunity for the four of them to become "family." Now that was a thought that had never crossed her mind before. That would actually be reaching far out of her comfort zone. *Am I ready for that? Ready or not, here I come.*

Lizzy lay in bed rehearsing over and over in her mind, this morning's conversation with her son. This could be exciting. Life could be exciting again as she had recently found out by starting to draw again. She tried to close her eyes and sleep, but sleep wouldn't come.

It was good to have guests back at Haleub Place again. It was a well-needed diversion to get everybody's focus back on others instead of themselves. The Reeds were a jovial family. Glen had a quick wit, which kept everybody laughing at the dinner table. Their oldest son, Matthew, had just turned five and had a very refreshing way of putting things. Upon noticing the barometer hanging on the wall at the entrance to the dining room, he pointed and said as serious as could be, "I've never seen a 'two clockter' before."

Trying to hide his amusement, Marshall responded by saying, "It's amazing, isn't it, Matthew? One dial lets us know the temperature, and the other lets us know the amount of moisture in the air."

Heather had her hands full with their other son, Seth, who was three. She was trying to teach him some table manners, like how not to eat with his fingers.

Seth turned to Marcus. "What kind of shoes do you have?"

Startled and amused by the question, he paused for a minute.

"Color will do," offered Heather, smiling sheepishly.

"He looked down at his feet before answering. "Brown. I have brown shoes, Seth. What kind of shoes do you have?"

"I have brown shoes too."

"Well then, we match, don't we, Seth?" he said matter-of-factly.

Seth just looked up and kept eating his biscuit.

As they got out of the car, Julia hurried over to her friend. "Are you all right, Kate?"

"No, not really." She sniffed.

"What's wrong? What happened?" she said as they walked to the door.

"It's Mr. Thompson," she said, trying to keep back the tears. "He's had a stroke."

"Oh, no!" Julia cried.

"What's going on?" her grandfather asked Julia as he stepped inside the door to the hallway.

"Mr. Thompson, the gardener at Haleub Place, has had a stroke," she explained.

One look at Kate let him know that she was in a fragile state of shock right now. "Come here," he said as he stepped toward her. "You need a hug." As he wrapped his strong arms around Kate, he felt the dam burst. Her whole body trembled as she wept silently in his arms. Mrs. Benton had gone into the living room for a moment and returned carrying with her a box of tissues. She pressed a couple into Kate's hand.

Mr. Benton stood there steady for Kate until she stopped trembling. Somehow, he knew that these tears were not just for Mr. Thompson, but a release for pent-up feelings triggered by the news of the stroke. "Let's go sit in the living room," he suggested to everyone as he walked Kate to the couch where Julia sat down.

"What else did your letter say? How's he doing now?" asked Julia.

"My eyes got too blurry with tears," she said as she wiped her eyes with the tissues. "I never finished reading the letter. Mr. Thompson is in a room in the house, and there is a new gardener living in the garden house." She wiped her eyes again with the tissues and blew her nose. "I'll read the rest of the letter later when I calm down some more."

"I'm sorry that your first news from home was so upsetting," said Mrs. Benton, trying to comfort her. "I'm sure the rest of your letter will explain more to you." She stood up from her chair, "You and Julia spend some time together while I go put away the groceries."

"I'll help you, dear," said her husband. "Are there any more things left in the car? I know I forgot to get my things out of the trunk."

"I think I've got everything, but you can check when you go out. Thank you."

Kate felt better now that she had released her emotions. She sighed. "Thanks for being here for me. You are my dearest friend, Julia."

Julia leaned over and gave her a big hug. They hung on to each other for a few moments. "Like my grandfather said, 'Sometimes, you just need a hug.'"

Marcus sat in on the business meeting with his uncle and Mr. Reed. His uncle had told him, "The way to learn the business is to do the business." He was to be a part of every business meeting, and with that responsibility, there would be compensation. Again, his uncle's thoughts were, "The best way to learn to handle finances was to have some finances to handle."

The whole household thoroughly enjoyed the Reed family's visit, and they were encouraged to come back soon for another visit. Just as they were driving away, Mr. Wagner pulled into the parking area with his things ready to unload. "Here, let me give you a hand with your things, Mr. Wagner," Marcus offered as he got out of his car.

"Thank you," he said, smiling. "You can call me Walter if you'd like."

"Well, welcome to the Haleub Place family, Walter," Marcus said as he extended his hand.

"Yes, welcome, Walter. We're glad to have you with us," added Mr. Jules.

"Thank you, both. I'm very glad to be here. This opportunity couldn't have come at a better time."

"Let's take the first load," suggested Marcus, "and come back for the rest with the wheelbarrow. It worked well to move Mr. Thompson's things that way."

"Good idea, sounds like a good plan."

As soon as they had moved all the things to the garden house, Marcus excused himself and headed back to the house to find his uncle.

"Knock, knock," he said as he appeared in the study doorway.

"Come in, what's on your mind?"

"I was wondering if I could run something by you for your advice." He held the letter to Mr. and Mrs. Williams in his hand.

"Have a seat." He gestured to the armchair in front of his desk.

"It takes a bit of explaining first." He took a deep breath and began. "After you told me where I was born the other day, it got me to thinking about my father. I've been wondering about him for a long time, but didn't know how to bring the subject up without causing a stir."

His uncle sat there calmly listening intently to every word.

"I went to Hamilton one day and looked up both my birth certificate and my father's. His parents' names and address were listed, so I copied the information down so I could try and make contact with them. The rest is explained in this letter which I am asking you to read before I send it." And with that, he handed the letter to his uncle.

His uncle read the letter carefully, looked up at Marcus and nodded, and then read it one more time. "It's a very good letter. I think you should send it," he said, handing it back to him. "Just one question. Why did you think this would cause 'a stir'?"

"I didn't know how mother would take it, and I didn't want anyone, especially you, to think that I was ungrateful for everything that's been done for me."

Marshall was silent for a moment as he studied Marcus's face. "Just for the record, no one, especially me, would think you are ungrateful for anything. Actually, we are all grateful for what you've brought to us. The other is just honest curiosity any of us would have if we were in your shoes."

Marcus breathed a sigh of relief. "This, as well as talking to Mother the other day, was a lot easier than I thought it would be."

"You don't have to hesitate to talk to me about anything, Marcus. You are loved. You are family. That's what family is for."

His uncle shifted in his chair as he studied Marcus' face for a moment. "Let me ask you something. Are there any specific questions that you feel will be answered by finding your father?

"I have a few questions to ask him, but the main one is why he left. Just meeting him will give me some idea of what he's like and what I'm made from. Being aware of his pitfalls could possibly help me to avoid them."

"You are on the right track in reaching out to your father's parents. Maybe we can all work together to see if we can uncover anything about your father."

"That would be great, Uncle Marshall! Thank you so much. I'll get this letter in the mail today."

"How does your mother feel about all this?"

"She's okay with me contacting my grandparents, but I don't know what she would say about looking for information about my father. We didn't talk about that part. She encouraged me to talk to you about all this."

When Mr. and Mrs. Benton returned to the living room after putting their purchases away, they found Julia and Kate much more relaxed than before.

"Anyone up for a game of dominoes?" Julia's grandfather asked with a wide grin and expectant eyes.

"Sure," said Julia, smiling. "I thought you'd never ask." Looking at Kate, she asked, "Are you ready for this?"

"I guess so," she answered hesitantly.

"Good," he said, "let's play at the kitchen table."

They all moved to the kitchen, and Mr. Benton began to explain the game to Kate. "All the facedown dominoes are divided equally among players, similar to dealing out cards. The player that has the double blank, places it in the center of the table to begin the game. The others, in turn, try to match an end of their domino to what has been laid down. Doubles are always laid at right angles to the other dominoes. The game continues until someone plays all their dominoes. The next round starts with the double ones and so on until the last round starts with double sixes. You'll catch on pretty quickly once we start playing."

The game went pretty smoothly, and just as Mr. Benton had hoped, everyone was laughing again. This was the needed diversion from the seriousness that the letter had brought earlier. With the last round played and the points tallied up, Mr. Benton declared, "We have a winner! Our new champion is Kate Silverton!"

With this, came chuckling from both Julia and her grandmother.

"What's so funny?" Kate asked mystified.

"Just wait a minute, it's coming," said Julia.

"What's coming?"

Mr. Benton reached behind him to the cabinet where they kept the games. He pulled out a homemade trophy of a larger-than-life double six domino. It was made out of wood, painted black with white dots. He presented this to Kate with flourish.

Kate laughed with the rest of them. "So this is what you've been chuckling about."

"Yes. He loves it when there's somebody new playing who doesn't know about the trophy," said his wife. "It has brought much amusement over the years, especially when the new person wins."

"Maybe everybody would like to play after dinner tonight?"

"We'll see, dear. Let Kate enjoy her trophy a bit before someone else wins and you take it away from her."

"Let's go sit on the porch swing for a while," Julia suggested to Kate. "Let us know if we can help you with dinner, Grandmother. We'll be right out front."

"Thanks, girls. I'll let you know."

"That was fun," said Kate as she let the screen door snap shut behind her.

"That's why I like coming here so much. My grandparents are a lot of fun."

They sat for a while just looking out at the beautiful countryside. The gentle squeak of the porch swing going back and forth.

"Maybe I can read the rest of my letter now." Pulling the letter from her pocket, she unfolded it and began again. "Mr. Thompson is gaining his strength back little by little…" she read out loud. "He's sitting up in bed, and they are getting a wheelchair so he can sit outside and get some fresh air… Mr. Wagner is the new gardener…" She turned to the second page and continued reading some of the parts out loud. When she was finished, she folded the letter back up to put in the envelope. "That was nice of him to send a letter letting me know about Mr. Thompson."

"Him? Who is that letter from?" questioned Julia. I thought it was from your mother."

"This letter is from Marcus. He said he saw my letter to Mother in the stack of mail one day and copied down the address. With so much going on, he didn't know if she had had a chance to write back yet, so he thought he would fill me in on what's been happening."

"How did he sign it?"

"Just 'Marcus.'"

Anna was chuckling as she washed up the dishes from breakfast. Ellen walked through the kitchen with the linens from the guest room. Due to the young ages of the children, the Reeds had all stayed in one room with two extra cots set up

"What's so funny?" she asked as she heard Anna chuckling.

"That little Seth. When his father pointed out the full moon last night, he said, 'The moon must have eaten a big dinner.'" They both chuckled over that one.

Still laughing, Ellen added, "My favorite is the 'two clockter' Marcus told us about."

"That is, a good one," agreed Anna, shaking her head in amusement. "When you get a chance, would you mind checking in on Mr. Wagner to see if he needs anything?"

"Sure, I'll be glad to. I'll get this laundry started and then head to the garden house."

"Make sure he knows he can come up for meals, guests or no guests. With sitting with Gil so much, I haven't got to talk to him much. As soon as we get a wheelchair, Gil can join us here in the kitchen if he's up to it."

"That would be great for him and Mr. Wagner to get to know each other. They could help each other out until he's more acquainted with the place."

Lizzy decided not to visit for a while until things settled down at Haleub Place. She was glad to help out last time, but Anna always wanted to do extra for her visits, and this way there would be minimal extras until Kate was back to help out in the kitchen and with the guest rooms.

Marcus promised to let her know if the Williamses contacted him. She was eager to know what might develop from all of this. Marcus was brave, far more courageous than she had ever been. It had simply never occurred to her to see if there were any grandparents who might be blessed to know they had a grandson.

Why did it take so long for her to recognize the value of family? Speaking of family, she hadn't seen her mother since Marcus's graduation. This would be a good time to go visit her to check up on how she was doing. Her neighbors had always been good to her, but maybe she should take more initiative and be more active in her mother's life.

Perhaps she could sketch her mother? Lizzy made a mental note to visit her mother at least once a month. Why had it taken her so long to come out of her cocoon? Most weekends she was home by herself, not really interacting with anybody.

Chapter 12

Mr. Williams sorted through the stack of mail the postman had just laid on the counter. All but one were addressed to Williams Repair Shop. He pulled out the one addressed to *Mr. and Mrs. James Williams* and carefully opened it. After reading through it twice, he folded it back up, put it in the envelope, and laid it aside.

When he came home that evening, without a word, he quietly laid the envelope on the table by Evelyn's place. She was cooking dinner and he knew she would see it soon enough. As he went to wash up, Evelyn began filling their plates, which she would bring to the table like she always did. It was at this point, he knew she would notice the letter.

"What's this?" she said as he sat down at the table across from her.

"It was delivered at the shop today."

She picked up the envelope, carefully pulled the letter out, and began reading. Not looking up, she said, "You never mentioned to me about a young man stopping by the store asking about Mitchell."

Making no comment, James took another bite of his supper while she continued reading. Not sure of his own feelings about the letter, he was eager to hear what his wife had to say. She read the letter three times before she gently laid it on the table.

"James…" Her voice trembled. "We have a grandson. What's he like? Does he look like Mitchell?"

Taking his last bite of supper, he paused as he looked up at her. "He was only in the store a few minutes, and I didn't know who he was at the time." Her eyes began to moisten as she listened. "I was so startled by his question that I didn't know quite how to answer him. I told him I hadn't seen Mitchell in over twenty years. He thanked me and left the store."

"We have to answer his letter, James. We have to…"

"I know. I just don't know what to say."

"Maybe we should invite him to come to the house for dinner?"

"Maybe you could write the letter and sign both our names."

"Let me think about it and see what I can put together."

By now, her supper was cold, so she took it back to the kitchen to warm it up. Still dazed by the news, she whispered softly to herself, "I'm a grandmother. I have a grandson."

Lizzy spent the next weekend with her mother. "Do you mind if I sketch you, Mother?"

"No, not at all. When did you start that up again?"

"Several weeks ago. One day I got the urge to stop by the art supply store and pick up a few things, and I've been sketching ever since."

"Have you been to Haleub Place lately?"

"Not since right after Gil had a stroke."

"Gil had a stroke? How is he doing? Can I talk while you sketch?"

"Yes, you can talk while I sketch," she assured her. "Marcus says he is stronger now and can sit up in bed for a while. They moved him up to the house so they could keep an eye on him. Anna has been with him night and day until recently."

"Gil's been with the Jules family as long as I can remember, Lizzy. He must be in his eighties by now."

"Anna's not much younger than Gil. It's a good thing Ellen is there to help out."

"And a good thing Kate is there to help her mother as well."

"Well, that's the reason I'm keeping my visits to a minimum right now," Lizzy explained as she continued sketching. "Kate is away for the summer with Julia and that in addition to Anna looking after Gil, leaves everyone else juggling jobs and responsibilities."

"Is Marcus taking care of the grounds now?" her mother asked.

"He was until Uncle Marshall found someone to take over for him. A Mr. Wagner is living in the garden house now, and according to Marcus, he seems to know what he's doing. Having him around takes a load off of everybody else and when Kate gets back next month things should be settling down especially since she's graduated from high school now."

"It's hard to imagine Haleub Place without Gil puttering around in the gardens. Have you met Mr. Wagner?"

"Just briefly. He's a very nice man and comes highly recommended."

"I guess some changes are inevitable." She sighed. "When Connie passed on, I couldn't imagine going to Haleub Place without her being there, but when I met Marcus, I couldn't imagine not going. Some changes add a richness to our lives, we never could have imagined."

"Funny you should bring that up, Mother." She paused, not knowing how to continue. "Marcus has recently located his other set of grandparents on his father's side. I never met Mitch's parents. Marcus has written a letter to them, but as far as I know has not heard back from them yet."

"Well, Lizzy, you are just full of surprises today, between your taking up drawing again and all the news from Haleub Place. Are you almost finished, I mean with your sketch?"

"Yes," she said, "I'm almost done."

"How do you feel about Marcus finding his grandparents?"

"At first I didn't know what to think about it. I remembered you telling me how blessed you were when you first found out about Marcus. It honestly never occurred to me to even think about Mitch's parents, much less try to locate them. Actually, Marcus was trying to find out anything he could about his father and that led him to his grandparents still living in Hamilton, which is where I was living with Mitch and where Marcus was born."

She laid her pencil down and handed the sketch-book to her mother.

"That's wonderful, Lizzy! You have a real talent for this!" She held up the book. "Do you have others in here that I can look at?"

"Yes, there are several in there."

Emelia slowly flipped through the pages, studying each one with great care. It was so wonderful to see her daughter take an interest in drawing again. She had shown much promise in school, and these were no exception.

"These are good, Lizzy, very good," she said as she handed the book back to her daughter. "Are you hungry? Would you like a bite to eat?"

"Yes, Mother, I am, but please let me help fix something." She got up and followed her mother into the kitchen. "What if you tell me how to make it, and I do all the work? That way you can rest and I can learn how to cook something different."

"Well, since you put it that way, how can I resist? Let's start with something simple like meat loaf, baked potatoes, and green bean casserole."

"My mouth is watering already. What first?" Lizzy asked.

Kate received another letter in the mail. "You sure are popular around here." Julia laughed. "You get more mail here than I do." She leaned in close to her friend. "And who is this one from?" she teased.

Kate opened the letter and looked to see who signed it before she started reading. "This one really is from my mother." They both broke into laughter.

At lunch, Julia's grandfather addressed the girls. "Is there anything you girls would like to do while you're here? You'll be leaving in almost two weeks. I don't know where the summer went," he said, scratching his head. "It will be awfully quiet around here when you two go home."

The girls looked at each other, and Julia spoke up. "Could we go into town for ice cream again and go to a few shops?"

"Yes, I'd like to get a few things to take back with me to remember my time here with you this summer," added Kate.

"Hazel, do you have any errands to run in town?" Her husband asked as he tried to think of anything he needed as well.

"Let me think about it for a minute. I'm sure I can come up with something."

By the end of lunch, they had come up with enough errands to warrant a trip to town. After helping to clear the dishes from the table and put things away in the kitchen, the girls excitedly went upstairs to get ready to go to town.

This had been a wonderful time for the girls to be able to spend this much time together. Julia would be looking for a job when she got home. She had been given the opportunity to go to college, but chose not to at this time.

While they were hurriedly getting ready, Kate stopped for a moment. "What if you came to stay at Haleub Place for a while, Julia? From what my mother and Marcus said, they could probably use some help."

"No way," replied Julia. "I would love to, but I'm not going to get in the way of what you and Marcus have going right now. Outside of summers, this will be the first time neither of you have been in school at the same time."

"Well, you could come to visit from time to time, couldn't you?"

"I'd like that, Kate, but I've got a feeling that both of our lives are about to change, yours with Marcus and mine with I'm not sure what."

"Are you girls ready?" Mr. Benton called upstairs.

"We'll be right down," answered Julia as they both grabbed their purses and took one last look at themselves in the mirror.

Evelyn sat down to write to Marcus. What do you say to a grandson you've never met? It was evident that he wanted to connect or he wouldn't have made the first move by sending a letter to them.

Dear Marcus,

What a joy to discover that we have a grandson! Thank you so much for writing to us. We would love to meet you and get to know you. Please come to dinner next Sunday at two o'clock. Looking forward to seeing you soon.

With love,

James and Evelyn Williams

As she sat there, pen in hand, Evelyn thought back to when Mitch was a young boy. Looking at the pictures hanging on their wall, she wondered what went wrong. His smile at age five revealed a missing tooth. At ten he was holding a fishing pole in one hand with his catch still hanging on the hook at the end of the fishing line. The other picture taken by a school photographer reflected a more serious look at age sixteen.

What was beneath the tough exterior that had developed in the last few years of school? She had gone over this a thousand times in her mind over the last twenty years and each time came up empty. What had caused him to move out so abruptly after graduation? Where was he now? Was he even alive? Were there any other grandchildren out there? There was no end to the questions, the torment over the years of not knowing… of not knowing anything.

For a few years, they had heard little bits of information passed on to them through parents of a few of his friends they would run into from time to time. In time, that stopped as their inquiries were met with continued replies that no one had seen or heard of him in a while. He just disappeared. Apparently, from what Marcus relayed, even his wife had no idea of where he was or why he left.

They would meet Marcus first and then determine from that the possibility of meeting his mother. *One step at a time*, she reminded herself as she rose from the table with the letter in hand to mail.

For the last few days, Marcus had divided his time between business and gardening. The mornings were full helping Mr. Wagner harvest vegetables, and the afternoons were spent studying some business contracts his uncle had given him to look over.

Marcus lay in bed waiting for sleep to come. His body was tired, but his mind was in full gear. He didn't expect a reply from Kate. It would be nice, but she would be home soon and they could talk then. What a whirlwind life had become since graduation. The summer he had envisioned concentrating on learning the business, had not turned out quite as he had expected. Between Gil's declining health, the arrival of Mr. Wagner, and the search for his father turning up his grandparents, the summer was almost gone and soon Kate would be added to the mix.

They all had been juggling responsibilities at Haleub Place over the summer and now with Mr. Wagner moved in, he would have more time for the business as the weight of the grounds keeping would be lifted off him. Kate would be able to help her mother and perhaps Anna could slow down and spend more time with her brother.

At a loss as to where to go next with his search for his father, Marcus was eager to meet his grandparents. They could tell him about the younger years growing up, and he was hoping to be able to see some pictures of his father as his mother had none to show him. Uncle Marshall had suggested that they wait until after Marcus had met his grandparents to see if they could gather any leads from them as to where to start looking. It was hard to turn his thoughts off, but sleep eventually came and the next thing he heard was the sound of birds chirping as the sun rose on another day.

Tomorrow, he would be meeting with his grandparents. It helped that he had at least briefly met his grandfather, but he was a bit anxious about the whole thing. The letter he had received from them was short but very encouraging.

Ellen was looking forward to Kate coming home next week. Though she was glad for Kate to have had the time with Julia at her grandparents, she missed her company even more than her help. In the absence of Kate's father, the two had grown quite close to each other. Their relationship had moved beyond just mother and daughter to the companionship of friends. Someday she knew Kate would most likely find someone of her own and this time apart from each other was a good preparation for them both.

It was becoming evident that Anna needed to spend time on a regular basis with her brother, Gil. Ellen had taken on more and more of the planning and preparation in the kitchen this summer in addition to the upkeep of the house and guestrooms. She would need to talk with Mr. Jules and Kate about whether Kate could be in a more full-time position to help or whether someone else was needed to step in for Anna, just as Mr. Wagner had stepped in for Gil. Things seemed to be rapidly changing all around Haleub Place, a shifting, a changing of the guard so to speak.

Chapter 13

Marcus held in his hand the directions to his grandparents' house. He had saved the paper where the waiter had written them down weeks ago at the restaurant. Sycamore Street should be the next street on the right. He took a deep breath as he neared his turn. His palms were sweaty where he had gripped the steering wheel. "Relax," he told himself.

It was a modest home, part red brick and the rest, wood siding painted white with a forest green front door and window shutters. He parked the car and started up the sidewalk to the front door. His mix of emotions took him back to the day he had arrived at Haleub Place. Excitement and anticipation mixed with a large dose of the unknown.

His hand reached to lift the doorknocker, and he rapped sharply on the door twice. What seemed an eternity was only a matter of seconds before the door slowly opened. His grandfather, recognizing him from their earlier brief encounter stretched out his arm toward Marcus.

"Come in," he said as they shook hands.

As Marcus stepped inside, he met his grandmother walking toward him from the kitchen. "Oh, Marcus."

She stretched out her arms and gave him a big hug. As they stood there embracing one another, Marcus was amazed at how just walking through a door could open up a whole new world of family. For a brief moment, they all just stood there looking at each other.

"Let's all sit down in here for a minute," she said as she gestured to the living room. "Dinner's almost ready. Can I get you something to drink?" His grandmother sat down in one of the two chairs separated by the small table already holding someone's drink.

"A glass of water would be wonderful," answered Marcus as he sat down on the couch across from the chair.

She disappeared into the kitchen for a moment and soon returned holding two tall glasses of water. She handed one to Marcus and then sat in the matching chair on the other side of the table. "It's so good to meet you, Marcus," she said, smiling. "We were so surprised to receive your letter. I'm so glad you took the time to write to us."

"I'm sorry it took me so long to connect with you. I wish that I had reached out sooner." As he glanced around the room, his eyes rested on the three pictures hanging on the wall. "Is that my father? I've never seen any pictures of him before."

"That's him," his grandfather said quietly, nodding his head. "You favor one another. What made you come looking for us?" he said rather bluntly.

"As I said in my letter, I've been curious to find out anything I can about my father. When you told me, that day in the shop, that you hadn't seen him in over twenty years, I didn't know what else to say. The more I thought about it when I got home that day, the more I wanted to meet you both." He paused. "You see, I was twelve before I met my great-uncle and my grandmother for the first time. It changed my whole life when I met my mother's family, so I was willing to take the chance to meet you."

"It's going to take some getting used to," his grand-father said, "but I'm glad you reached out to connect, as you put it."

Mrs. Williams rose from her chair. "I'll go check on the dinner," she said as she went to the kitchen.

"It's nothing against you, Marcus," he continued, "but seeing you all of a sudden brings back a lot of memories, especially as you favor your father so much."

"I was concerned about that and hoped that what-ever might be stirred up would be for good and not for bad." They sat there in silence a few moments as Marcus intently studied the pictures of his father hanging on the wall.

"Dinner's ready," his grandmother's voice inter-rupted the silence.

Mr. Williams got up and headed to the dining room with his glass in hand. Marcus followed bringing his glass as well.

Lizzy enjoyed spending the weekend with her mother, especially the cooking lesson. This, in addition to help-ing Ellen in the kitchen at Haleub Place a few weeks ago, gave her incentive to try some new recipes. She had grown so accustomed to her routine at home that she rarely did anything different, including cooking. It was get up, go to work, come home, go to bed, and then do it all over again the next day.

She gazed out the window as the train carried her home. Tomorrow she would go to the grocery store and try something new. She began to make mental notes of the new items she would purchase. So far, this summer had been full of surprises. First it was wanting to draw again, and now she was actually wanting to cook, and something new at that. For the first time, Marcus had come by to visit and talk with her. *What would be next?* she wondered. *What was it that had started this new chain of events anyway?*

Her thoughts took her back to the dream she had had the day before Marcus's graduation and the conversation she had had with Uncle Marshall. He was right. She had harbored a lot of anger and bitterness toward Mitch. From the moment she let go of all that, her life had been different. The hurt and the anger had held her captive far too long. Now she was free to discover who she was.

Could this in any way be connected to Marcus wanting to know about his father? she wondered. Would he have felt at liberty to ask her about him before her "release" as she had decided to call it? Would she have projected her bitterness toward Mitch on his parents? Only now was she beginning to understand the extent to which bitterness can poison innocent parties.

Each morning, Walter and Marcus had something different to bring to Ellen in the kitchen. "I hope this isn't too much for you, Mrs. Silverton," Walter said as he set down two big baskets of fresh-picked green beans.

"No, not at all." She said, as she looked up from kneading her dough. "Anna can snap these while she's in Gil's room. She's always looking for something to do while she sits with him. And please, call me Ellen."

"Only if you call me Walter."

"I can do that," she said, smiling, "Walter."

"By the way, how is Mr. Thompson doing? Do you think it would be okay if I visited him? Maybe he could give me some pointers about what's where and how he tended to everything. Marcus has told me a lot already, but I thought it might help to get to know him and let him have some input into things around here."

"I'll ask Anna and get back with you on that at lunchtime."

"Marcus and I will bring some squash and tomatoes with us then. I'll let you get back to your dough, and I'll go catch up with Marcus. He's a hard worker and really knows what he's doing."

"That's for sure. You can always count on Marcus," she replied as she started kneading again. She caught herself following Walter with her eyes as he headed out the kitchen door. *I wonder what Kate will think about all the changes here when she gets back next week.*

Mr. Williams sat in his usual spot at the end of the table. "You can sit over there," he said as he pointed to the chair on his right, across from his wife's usual spot.

"Thank you so much for inviting me over for dinner," Marcus said as his grandmother set the serving dishes down on the table.

"We're glad to have the opportunity to get to know you," she said with a smile as she sat down at the table. "Go ahead, help yourself!" she encouraged him as she gestured to the dishes set before him.

"You mentioned in your letter that you and your mother had some difficult years and that you were living with your great-uncle. What happened that caused you and your mother to live apart from each other?" questioned his grandfather.

Marcus took a deep breath. Somehow, he knew this question would come up, and he had prepared in his mind how to answer.

"No disrespect to either of you," he said as he looked each of them in the eye. "My mother said that she and Mitch had not been married long before he started staying out all night from time to time. One night he came home to get his clothes, left, and never came back." He paused to take a few bites of his dinner and then continued.

"It was not too long after he left that my mother discovered she was pregnant with me. For years she struggled with trying to care for me as well as working to provide for us both. One day, she just never came to pick me up from the family she had left me with while she was at work. I stayed with them for a while until one day I came home from school and they had moved. The house was vacant and I had nowhere to go. After checking all the windows, I found one unlocked, so I climbed in through the window and stayed there by myself."

Both of his grandparents listened intently, not saying a word. He took a few more bites and picked up where he had left off.

"By this time, I was about twelve years old. One day I asked the groundskeeper at school if he could use any help. He let me help him after school and paid me for the work I did. That is what I bought food with, and the rest I saved up for a train ticket to Haleub Place. In a passing conversation, I had overheard someone mention it and for some reason felt drawn to go there. As soon as I had saved up enough money, I bought a ticket and just showed up one day. I asked the groundskeeper there if he needed any help, and he took me in, giving me room and board in exchange. It wasn't until months later that I learned that my great-uncle lived there.

"He hadn't seen my mother in over fifteen years but was able to find her and get us connected again. We all agreed that it would be best for me to live with my uncle, and he saw to it that I had a good education. In fact, I just graduated from college a couple months ago."

Figuring that he had said enough for now, Marcus took a few more bites of his dinner. It was silent for a while as his grandparents let all this sink in.

"Would you like some more?" his grandmother offered as she passed the potatoes. "There's plenty. Please, help yourself."

Marcus filled his plate again hoping that someone else would do the talking while he ate. Except for the clinking of silverware on dishes, there was awkward silence throughout the rest of the meal.

Finally, his grandfather raised his head and cleared his throat. With misty eyes, he looked straight at Marcus. "Son, I'm sorry you had to go through all that. I wish we could have been there for you."

His grandmother nodded, deep compassion in her eyes. Marcus was touched by their genuine caring. He certainly hadn't foreseen this kind of reception. It was humbling how they cared so much about someone they had just met. He wasn't sure how to respond.

"You had no way of knowing," he managed to say.

"We can't change the past, but if you are willing, your grandmother and I would like to be part of your future."

"Yes, Marcus, you are welcome here anytime," his grandmother added.

"Thank you so much for letting me stay with you this summer," Kate said as she gave Mr. and Mrs. Benton a big good-bye hug.

"Yes, thank you so much. We had a wonderful time together with you," echoed Julia.

"It was our pleasure, girls," said Grandmother Benton as she gave Julia a hug.

"It's going to be awfully quiet around here without you two," her husband added as he hugged her good-bye.

The girls were traveling together on the train until they reached Sandy Falls where they would part ways—Julia heading to Whispering Hills and Kate to Haleub Place. They boarded the train with their suitcases, Kate held the quilt Mrs. Benton had given her under one arm, and they both waved good-bye to Julia's grandparents as the train took off from the station.

"I'm so glad I got to spend the summer with you and your grandparents, Julia! Thanks for asking me!"

"I'm glad that you could come. It was great to be together again! I'm going to miss you when I get home."

"Julia, I wish for you to find a job that brings you joy as well as working with interesting people! My mother wrote that there may be an opportunity for me to help out on a more regular basis at Haleub Place if Anna decides to take leave for much needed rest as well as spend more time with her brother."

"And who knows what may develop between you and Marcus," Julia said, earnestly. "You've got to promise that you'll keep me posted on any developments."

Kate shifted in her seat. "I will, but give it some time. So much has happened since I've been away." She glanced out the window for a moment. "There's going to be a lot of changes to adjust to when I get home."

They both sat without speaking for a while watching the scenery go by. Finally, Julia broke the silence. "I sense that both of us are about to start a new chapter in our lives. Who knows what opportunities are just around the corner for us."

"I agree," said Kate as she let out a sigh and leaned her head back to rest on her seat. "I feel like we are both starting out on a new adventure."

Lost in their thoughts, the girls looked out the window as the train rolled on. Before they knew it, the conductor was calling out, "Next stop, Sandy Falls."

This was where Kate was getting off to catch another train that would take her to Haleub Place. With tears in their eyes, the girls hugged each other.

"I'm going to miss you, Kate. Promise me you'll write soon."

"I promise. I'm going to miss you too, Julia."

Kate stood, secured the bundled quilt under one arm, and picked up her suitcase. As she walked down the aisle to get off, she looked back at Julia and waved. As she heard the hiss of the train door close behind her, she sensed that one part of her life had come to a close and another was just beginning.

Looking up, she watched for Julia's face in the windows of the train as it passed by. They waved at each other one last time as the train pulled out of the station.

Kate slowly turned away from the empty tracks and walked toward the ticket window to check the schedule. She had a thirty-minute wait for her connecting train.

Finding an empty bench, she put her suitcase down and took a seat. Mentally she tried to prepare herself for the changes she would encounter in just a few short hours. Most likely, Marcus would be the one waiting at the station for her. They'd known each other as friends for the last ten years, but it would be different now that they were both open to be more than just friends. Since her train would be arriving late in the afternoon, she did not expect her mother to be with Marcus as she probably would be cooking dinner.

It was nice to have had the time away with Julia, but it would be good to be home again. She looked forward to the time she and her mother would spend catching up with each other. Then there was Mr. Thompson; she hoped he would be up to visitors tonight as she wanted to see for herself how he was doing. Sitting there lost in her thoughts, she remembered the sandwich Mrs. Benton had made for her. Kate reached for it in her bag and savored each bite as she waited for the train.

Chapter 14

Dear Marcus,

I am so thankful that you came into the repair shop that day and took the initiative to seek us out. It was good to be with you on Sunday, and we look forward to spending time with you in the future.

As I listened to you tell us about your childhood, it stirred up a lot of mixed feelings toward my son, your father. We, too, wonder what happened to Mitch. As I pondered all this after you left that night, it occurred to me that there was one contact I'd never considered before.

I have a younger brother, Nicholas, who sowed some wild oats in his last years of high school. His saving grace, so to speak, was enlisting in the armed forces right as he graduated from high school. He was stationed all over the world throughout his career and, when he retired, went back to visit some of those places.

It occurred to me that maybe Mitch might have tried to connect with his uncle Nick somewhere along the way. As a child, he loved to listen to stories his uncle told him of adventures he had in exciting *places. I have an address that forwards his mail to him wherever he happens to be staying at the time. We send Christmas cards to each other, but that's about all the contact we have.*

This morning, I sent a letter to my brother asking if he had heard from Mitch lately. I didn't mention you or your mother, but I did say that I had some important news for him. I'll let you know if I hear anything

In the meantime, please feel free to come by the shop or the house anytime you are in town.

Love,

Grandfather Williams

Letter in hand, Marcus headed down the hall to his uncle's study.

"Knock, knock," he said as he found the door already open.

Uncle Marshall looked up. "Come in." Noticing the opened letter in his nephew's hand, he said, "What's on your mind?"

"I just received a very interesting letter from my grandfather," he said as he handed the letter over to his uncle to read.

After reading the letter, Marshall looked up. "I agree, very interesting." He read the letter a second time and then handed it back to Marcus. "Depending on the response, this could make our search very easy," he said, pensively.

"That's what I thought too," Marcus nodded.

"It's up to you. Think about it for a while if you want to. We can wait to see what response your grandfather gets or we can start looking like we talked about a few days ago."

"Grandfather may not hear back for a matter of weeks, or even longer, and even then, his brother may not have a clue as to where my father is. Let's go ahead and get started like we talked about. The longer we wait, the longer it takes."

Ellen's eyes fluttered open as she glanced at the clock. She had been looking forward to this day for a long time. Kate was coming home. She had dearly missed her this summer, and they had so much to catch up on. Guests were expected today so she would be busy in the kitchen when Kate's train arrived. It would have been nice to meet her at the station, but Marcus would bring her home soon enough.

She smoothed back her wavy brown hair as she sat up in bed. A smile crept across her face as her feet touched the floor. Quickly, she got ready for the day and made her way into the kitchen. As she was fixing breakfast, she decided that today would be a good time to try and talk to Mr. Jules. Early on in the summer, Ellen had convinced Anna to let her handle breakfast by herself. That way Anna would have that responsibility lifted from her and could sleep a little longer or spend that time with Gil if he needed her.

Since Walter had moved into the garden house, he'd been coming up to the house for all his meals. Ellen was grateful for the company as the usual four for meals in the kitchen had been reduced to one, and she was not fond of eating alone. Anna had taken to eating her meals with Gil in his room. Kate would be home for dinner tonight, and that in itself would restore some sense of normality.

"Good morning, Ellen," Walter said as he entered the kitchen from the back door. Noticing the extra sparkle in her eyes, he added, "You sure seem extra cheerful this morning."

"Kate's coming home today," she said excitedly.

"That's right," he said, nodding his head. "She'll be in late this afternoon, won't she?"

"Yes. I can't wait for you to meet her."

"I'm looking forward to it."

Ellen fixed Anna's and Gil's tray, and Walter carried it down the hall to Gil's room. Early on, he had insisted on helping out in some way and this had become the normal routine for each meal. It was the least he could do to help out, and it had given him opportunity to spend a little time with both Anna and Gil on a regular basis. By the time he got back to the kitchen, Ellen had taken the serving dishes to the dining room, and then they both ate at the kitchen table together.

"What's the job for today, Walter?" Ellen inquired as usual.

"Today, I'm cleaning out all the old tomato vines. If I find any green tomatoes, I'll bring them in before lunch. The green beans are about done as well, though there might be a few left on the vine." He ate a few bites of breakfast. "This has been a good growing season, Ellen. Just the right amount of rain at the right time."

"You and Marcus certainly have brought in an abundant harvest. Very tasty, I might add."

"And you?" he asked. "How about your day?"

"Guests are expected this afternoon, so I'll be working on dinner and making sure the rooms are ready."

"Sounds like a full day for you and maybe a long night with you and Kate trying to catch up on each other." Finishing his last bite of breakfast, he wiped his mouth with the cloth napkin and then rolled it back up and placed it in the napkin ring. "I guess I'll be off," he said as he stood up to go. "Have a wonderful morning, Ellen,"

"You too, Walter."

Quickly she cleared the dining room table, cleaned up the kitchen, and then headed down the hallway. Mr. Jules would be home today because guests were coming. She knocked on his open study door.

"Excuse me, sir," she said gently.

Mr. Jules looked up from his desk. "Come in, Ellen," he said, smiling. "What can I do for you?"

"I was wondering if you had a few minutes."

"What's on your mind? Have a seat." He gestured to one of the chairs in front of his desk.

"Kate's coming home today, and I was wanting to ask you about maybe her helping out on a more full-time basis so Anna could have a well-deserved rest or maybe even the chance to be relieved of her duties if she chose to. I haven't said anything to Kate or Anna as I wanted to talk to you first." She shifted in her chair. "I'm concerned about Anna's health as well. She works so hard and this change in Gil's health has taken a lot out of her."

"Hmmm," he said, nodding his head in agreement. "You might have the perfect solution for Anna to be able to bow out gracefully." He sat there for a moment in thought and then continued. "Talk it over with Kate and see what she has to say and then let me know. If she's willing, the next hurdle will be convincing Anna to slow down."

Ellen was pleased that this conversation had gone so well.

"Excellent idea, Ellen. And by the way, you have done a wonderful job juggling all the cooking and housework as well! I know you'll be glad to have Kate home again. We all have missed her smiling face around here. I'm glad she had the time with Julia. They're great friends."

"Thank you, sir," she said as she stood up to leave. "I'll let you know what Kate says."

"Good. Thank you for the wonderful suggestion. It sounds like a good solution for everyone."

Ellen couldn't help but be excited about this proposition as she walked back to the kitchen to get busy cooking for the expected guests.

Kate was still chewing her last bite of sandwich when the train arrived. Quickly she gathered her things and boarded with the other travelers. Finding an empty seat by a window, she settled into the last leg of her journey. Just a few more hours and she would be home. Things would not be the same this year with no school to go to this fall. She was hoping she could work at Haleub Place and not have to go looking for a job somewhere.

She gazed out the window and let her mind go into neutral for a while. The scenery was beautiful changing from thick green forests to farmland and pastures. The seat next to her remained empty for the entire ride, giving her the quiet time she needed to transition from her two months vacation. All too soon, the scenery began to look familiar, and she realized the next stop was where she was getting off.

Searching from her window, she looked for a familiar face in the crowd waiting at the station. Her eyes suddenly lit up as she saw Marcus standing there waiting for her. He saw her too and a smile spread across his face. When the train came to a full stop, she quickly gathered her things and eased down the aisle in the line of passengers ready to disembark. When she came down the steps, Marcus quickly reached for her suitcase.

"It's so good to see you again, Kate," he said, hugging her with his free arm. "I've really missed you this summer."

"It's good to see you too, Marcus," she said as they started walking with the crowd toward the parking area. It felt good to have his arm resting on her shoulder. They had known each other for years, but this was the first time she had felt her heart beating so strongly in his presence.

"Your mother wanted to come with me to meet you at the station, but guests arrived earlier this afternoon and she is home cooking dinner. She really missed you this summer too."

"I missed her too, but I had a great time with Julia and her grandparents!" Kate looked up at Marcus. "How is Mr. Thompson doing? It was so sad to hear about his stroke."

"He's able to sit up now, and we have a wheelchair for him so he can sit outside on the front porch and get some fresh air. Compared to how you saw him last, he's pretty weak, but he's made a lot of progress from where he was right after his stroke."

As they approached the car, Marcus got the keys out to open the trunk for the luggage and then opened the passenger door for Kate. He waited while she got in and then closed the door and walked around to the driver's side. As he slid in the front seat, Marcus started the car and turned his head toward Kate. "So, tell me about your summer," he said as they drove off from the station.

"Julia and I had a great time! Her grandparents are a lot of fun. I learned how to quilt, how to play dominoes, watched her grandfather make bird houses, and of course, Julia and I got to spend every day with each other!"

"That's great that you have a friend like that. Since Jake and I started going to college, we haven't had as much time together."

"So, how was your summer?"

"Actually, it was pretty busy between learning the business with Uncle Marshall and helping Walter get caught up on the grounds. I also discovered my grandparents on my father's side. They don't live that far away, and they had me over for dinner one time."

"How did you get connected with your grandparents? I've never heard anybody even mention them before."

"While I was away at school, I started wondering about my father and determined in my mind that when I graduated, I would start looking for him." He paused and glanced at Kate.

"Uncle Marshall and I were in Hamilton one day, and he happened to mention that I was born there. I did a little research and found an address for my grandparents. I wrote to them explaining who I was and they invited me for dinner."

Kate looked at Marcus. "That's wonderful that you got to meet them." She looked perplexed. "I didn't know that you were looking for your father. Did you find him?

"No. No one seems to have heard from him for almost twenty years. Uncle Marshall is helping me to look for him. We have no leads as yet"

"I can understand your wanting to find out about your father and his family. My mother's parents live in town, and I only see them a few times a year." She looked out her window. "I haven't seen my father's family since his funeral."

"It's good to spend time with your family," said Marcus. "It gives you a window to see where you've come from and what you're made of. You can follow in their footsteps or make choices to take you in a different direction."

"I really enjoyed spending time at Julia's grandparents. It was very peaceful there and reminded me a little of Haleub Place. I had a great time, but it will be good to be home again."

"It is really good to see you again, Kate. I'm glad you're back," he said, glancing at her as he drove home. "This has been a very unusual summer. Nothing's been the same since you've been gone. Mr. Wagner moved in, and Mr. Thompson and Anna are not in their usual places. I've been stretched in a different direction trying to learn the business. There's just been a lot of adjustments to make all at once." He looked over at Kate again. "I hope we can spend more time together now that we're both out of school."

"I'd like that, Marcus," she said, smiling at him. "So, how is Mr. Wagner fitting in to all of this? What's he like?"

"He's a good worker and very knowledgeable about the grounds. As soon as Mr. Thompson was well enough for company, he started carrying the meal trays down to his room. That gave them a chance to talk and get to know each other and share information about the grounds. He's a gentle man like Mr. Thompson, and they get along very well. He's been very helpful to your mother as well, whenever she needs some help with something. I think you'll like him," he said, smiling.

Chapter 15

Lizzy looked up at the ceiling as she lay in bed. The moonlight was casting dancing shadows from the tree branches swaying gently in the breeze. All this stir about the Williamses had caused her to wonder what had really happened to Mitch. And what if Marcus found him, then what? Just when things seemed to be settling down for her and she was rediscovering who she was, this black hole seemed to be opening up. Making contact with Mitch's parents was one thing, but finding Mitch was something she was not sure if she was ready for.

Why was life so complicated? If only I could talk to Uncle Marshall about all this. He always has wisdom for every situation. Now that Kate's back home, I think I'll make plans to visit Haleub Place.

Lizzy was eager to visit. She especially wanted to hear firsthand from Marcus about his meeting with his grandparents. Depending on how they received him, she wondered how they might regard her. *Why is it that sometimes as soon as you let go of something, it flies back in your face?* It was so recently that she had gotten Mitch out of her system by letting go of the anger and bitterness toward him. Now it seemed like things were being stirred up again.

"Mother, it's so good to see you again," Kate said as she walked through the kitchen door.

Ellen stopped what she was doing and gave her daughter a big hug. As they embraced, she said, "It's good to have you home again, Kate. I've really missed you these past two months." Her eyes sparkled as she spoke. "I would have come with Marcus to get you at the station—"

"I know," Kate interrupted, "Marcus told me there were guests arriving today." She looked around the kitchen. "Dinner sure smells good!"

"It's almost ready. I'm just waiting on the rolls to brown before I put everything in serving dishes."

"Looks like I came at the right time. I'll just set my things in my room and come right back," Kate said.

"Here, let me help you with your suitcase," Marcus said as he reached for her luggage. He followed Kate down the hall and set her suitcase in their sitting room.

"Thank you, Marcus."

"Glad to be of help. I'll let you get settled and see you after dinner?" he asked expectantly.

"Sure," she replied.

"I'll see you later then," he said as he left the room to go meet the guests. As he walked down the hallway, he heard voices in the front room. As he entered the room, Marshall rose from his chair.

"Matthew, Sarah, I'd like you to meet my nephew, Marcus Williams."

"Nice to meet you," Marcus replied as they shook hands. He sat down in the chair facing the sofa they were sitting on.

"We've heard a lot of good things about you, Marcus," said Matthew. "Your uncle speaks very highly of you."

"Yes, he does," agreed Sarah.

"Well, thank you," said Marcus a bit embarrassed.

"I was just telling the Cookseys what a hard worker you are, always ready to lend a hand whenever you can."

"We're all here to help each other," he replied. "I figure that if I keep sowing good seeds, they'll bring a harvest back to me when I have a need."

"That's a good attitude to have," agreed Matthew. "I wish more people felt the same way you do." He shifted himself on the sofa. "Marshall tells me that since you've graduated, you've been working on learning the business."

"I have a wonderful teacher," he said as he gestured toward his uncle.

Just then, Ellen appeared in the doorway. "Dinner is ready."

As the middle-aged couple stood up, Marshall led the way to the dining room.

"Oh, that looks delicious," exclaimed Sarah as she saw the table spread with the serving dishes. The steam rising up carried the aroma of the savory food.

"It smells delicious too," echoed Matthew.

Kate carefully laid the quilt over the back of an armchair and then turned to put away her suitcase. When she finished, she started down the hall to the kitchen and met a man carrying two trays of food.

"You must be Kate," he said with a warm smile.

"Yes," she said, returning the smile. "You must be Mr. Wagner."

"Yes, welcome home. It's nice to meet you. I've heard many wonderful things about you."

"Thank you. Do you mind if I follow you to Mr. Thompson's room?"

"Not at all. Come on. Look who I found," Walter said as he set the tray down in Gil's room.

Gil glanced up.

"Hi, I'm back," she said. "How are you doing?"

"I'm doing much better, thank you. It's good to have you back, Kate." His voice sounding just as strong as she had remembered before. "We've sure missed your smiling face around here this summer," he said, reaching for her hand.

"Well, look who's back," came a voice from behind. Anna placed her arm around Kate's waist and pulled her close. "Welcome home, we sure have missed you this summer."

"Thank you. I've missed all of you too. It's good to be home again." She caught a whiff of their dinner tray. "Mother's probably waiting on us to get back to the kitchen for dinner. I'll let you eat your dinner while it's hot and come back and see you another time."

"You'd better," Gil said in jest.

"I promise," she said, and she and Mr. Wagner turned to go to the kitchen.

Ellen looked up as they came into the kitchen. "Well, I guess you've met each other," she said, beaming. "I'm just getting dinner on the table. You're just in time."

As they all sat down at the table, Walter exclaimed, "Dinner sure smells good, Ellen."

"It sure does," echoed Kate. "It's good to be home again."

As they filled their plates, Ellen asked, "How was the trip home?"

"Julia and I rode together for the first half and then we parted ways. The last few hours were rather quiet as I took a seat by the window and the seat next to me remained empty for the whole trip. Thank you for letting me go. I had a wonderful time. Sorry I wasn't here to help out when you were shorthanded."

"When Walter came"—Ellen looked toward him as she spoke—"we all pitched in together, and everything worked out. Marcus helped him, and Mr. Jules took a turn at sitting with Gil when needed. Even Lizzy helped out one weekend when she was here visiting."

Walter began eating as Kate and Ellen began to catch each other up on the news of the summer. He just smiled and nodded when appropriate and kept on eating. When his plate was empty, he rose from the table, plate in hand, and excused himself.

"It was delicious as usual, Ellen, and it was good to finally meet you, Kate. I've been hearing good things about you all summer. Have a nice evening, ladies," he said as he carried his plate to the counter and went out the back door.

After dinner, Marshall, Marcus and their guests sat out on the front porch to enjoy the late summer evening before sunset.

"What a lovely place you have here, Marshall," Sarah said, admiring the flowers that were in bloom out front.

"Who takes care of all this beauty?" inquired Matthew.

"Marcus has had a hand in it for the past ten years," replied Marshall.

"Most all of it was done by Mr. Thompson until he had a stroke a couple months ago," Marcus quickly added. "Mr. Wagner is taking care of things for us now."

"That couldn't be Walter Wagner, could it?" exclaimed Sarah.

Marshall leaned in with his head turned toward the Cookseys. "Yes, as a matter of fact, his name is Walter. How do you know of him?"

"He worked for our dear friends, Tom and Barb Sheffield, until Tom passed away recently. She didn't want to live in such a large house by herself and have the burden of having to keep it up. Mr. Wagner did a wonderful job of keeping the grounds for them. I'm sure he'll do the same for you."

Marshall was pleased. "He had excellent references, and you confirm what we have already discovered. He's a hard worker, knows what he's doing, and is a fine gentleman."

It was a lovely evening, the four of them sitting out on the porch together. Marcus recalled that it had only been a short time since everyone had been gathered there for his graduation celebration. It felt like much longer than that since he had been home. As the sun went down, a cool breeze began to stir, and the Cookseys decided to turn in for the night after stopping by the library to pick out a book to take back to their room.

"We'll see you in the morning?" They looked to Marcus.

"Yes, I'll meet you for breakfast," he assured them.

"Sleep well," added Marshall. "So glad you both could come visit."

Marcus excused himself and went to find Kate. He knocked on her door, and she quickly opened it.

"Come in."

"Would you like to go for a walk?" he said as he stepped into the room.

"Sure," she answered, her eyes sparkling.

"You might want to grab a sweater or a light jacket; there's a cool breeze stirring. I'll meet you in the kitchen in a few minutes. I'm going to go grab a jacket myself."

"Okay, see you in a minute."

"Who was that at the door?" her mother called out.

"It was just Marcus. We're going to go for a walk," she said as she found her jacket in the closet. "I'll be back later, Mother." She stepped out into the hallway and closed the door behind her. She walked to the kitchen and sat down on the bench near the table where there was a small lamp kept on all night. In no time, Marcus was back, and they went out the kitchen door together.

"I've been waiting all summer for you to get home, Kate," he said as they started down the path. "I've missed you very much…not just over the summer but through the whole school year."

Not knowing how to answer, Kate just looked at him. The moonlight cast its light on them as they headed in the direction of the pond.

"I remember my first time at the pond. Mr. Thompson had encouraged me to catch up with you and Jake and Julia. That was the first time I remember spending time with children close to my age other than just going to school."

"I remember that day," Kate replied, chuckling. "As I recall, you hardly said a word at all."

"It was pretty overwhelming for me. You three were my first friends ever!"

As they cleared the slight incline to the pond, the gentle breeze rippled the reflection of the full moon on the water. They sat down on the wooden bench together. Marcus stretched his arm across Kate's shoulder and pulled her close. Kate laid her head against his shoulder. Neither one spoke for some time as they sat there together in the quiet of the evening.

Finally, Marcus broke the silence. "Kate, I've thought a lot about you especially this senior year. Now that we've both graduated, I don't want to take the chance of you going away somewhere. I was hoping that when I came home, you might want to be more than just friends. I realized how much you mean to me, and I hoped that you might feel the same way about me." He was silent for a moment, giving her time to think about what he had just said.

With her heart pounding, Kate spoke slowly. "Marcus, I've always enjoyed spending time with you. I remember the first time I met you and how quiet you were. Then Jake and Julia came for a visit and you started to open up a bit. Over the years, it's been nice having a big brother like you around." She was quiet for a minute and then continued.

"I was sure you would find some nice girl when you went off to college, and I was content to be your friend. Even at your graduation, I expected you to introduce us all to that special girl you had found at school."

Shifting her gaze from across the lake, Kate turned her head to look up at the stars. "When I started getting your letters this summer, I knew something was up because you never sent me letters the whole time you were away at school."

Marcus laughed softly. "Was it that obvious? I was waiting until I got home to talk to you. It turned out that you left so soon there was no time to talk. I was resolved to wait a couple more months, and then Mr. Thompson had a stroke." He shifted on the bench. "I knew you cared as much about him as I did, and I felt like I had to tell you. The fact is, Kate, I really missed you, especially at that time." He leaned his head down to kiss the top of her head. "I hope you don't have any plans to go away again anytime soon."

"No, I don't. As a matter of fact, Mother was talking to me after dinner about stepping in on a full-time basis around here so Anna can spend her time with her brother and take a well deserved rest. This would keep me here rather than having to go somewhere else to find work. According to your uncle and my mother, it might be the only way that Anna would agree to slowing down. She's such a dear woman that if she saw it would be a help to me, she might readily agree to the plan."

"I think they're right, Kate. It sounds like a wonderful plan, especially the part about you staying right here!" he said as he pulled her close and patted her shoulder.

Content to sit in silence, the two watched the reflection of the moon on the pond. It was a peaceful night. The stars shone brightly, and only sounds of crickets and the occasional bull frog could be heard.

A yawn slipped out from Kate and Marcus straightened up on the bench. "We should probably head back to the house. You've had a long day, Kate and I'm sure you're tired after your long trip."

"Yes, all the excitement of the day is about to catch up with me. I think I'm ready to call it a night."

They rose from the bench together, and Marcus reached for Kate's hand as they started down the path back to the house. The small lamp in the kitchen window gave light to them as they walked down the hall.

"I'll see you tomorrow, Kate," he said when they came to her door. "Sleep well."

"You too, Marcus," she said as she turned the knob. "Good night."

Chapter 16

"Hello, Mother," Lizzy said as she gave her mother a big hug. "It's good to see you again. I'm here for my next cooking lesson." She chuckled.

Emelia laughed. "Have you made any meatloaf lately?"

"Yes, as a matter of fact, I have. Green bean casserole too," she added as she sat down on the sofa.

"Lizzy, it's so good to see you," she said as she lowered herself gently onto the overstuffed chair. "Are you thirsty? Would you like something to drink?"

"No thank you, Mother. I'm fine." Her brow furrowed as she looked at her more closely. "I noticed how gingerly you sat down in your chair. Are you in pain?"

"It's just my joints, dear. They don't move as easily as they used to. I guess that's one of the benefits of seniority. I'm just not as limber as I used to be." She smiled, never complaining. Lizzy had never known her mother to complain about anything.

"How do you do it, Mother?" she asked quizzically. "How is it that you never have cause to complain about anything?"

"It's not that I don't have the cause, I just choose to look for the bright side instead. It's all in how you look at things."

Lizzy drew her legs up under her on the couch and looked intently at her mother. "How do you keep such a good attitude?"

"I learned to let the bad things go, Lizzy, and hold on to what is good. Something good can be learned from every situation, even if the only thing that's learned is how not to do something."

"Hmmm," was all that Lizzy uttered as she sat lost in thought.

"Is there something on your mind, dear?"

"Sort of… Do you remember I mentioned that Marcus was to meet his other grandparents?"

"Yes. How did that go?"

"It went really well," she said as she turned her gaze to the window. "I'm very happy for him."

"The hesitation in your voice betrays you. You don't sound very happy."

"I am, really, I'm happy for him. The reason I hesitate is that together, they might actually find Mitch, and I'm not sure I'm ready for that."

Her mother nodded slowly, "I see." They both sat there in silence for a few moments. "Well, Lizzy, if they do find him, since you weren't a part of the search, you are not obligated to him in any way. If there is to be a reconnection, let him and Marcus work it out. If he finds any answers to his questions, I'm sure he'll share them with you. Just because he's found, if he's found, doesn't mean he's going to be a part of your life. You can't live in the 'what ifs.' You've got to live in the now."

"You're right, Mother. I can't live in the 'what ifs.' I've already spent too much of my life there, and it wasn't really living, it was merely existing."

"You have your drawing that has come back to life—"

"And my cooking," she interrupted with a chuckle.

"Yes, and your cooking," she agreed amusingly.

"Speaking of which, what's the cooking lesson for today?"

Ellen was awakened by the brightness of the room. She quickly glanced at the clock and sat up with a start. She had gotten to bed a little later than usual in all the excitement of Kate coming home. Hurriedly, she got dressed, and trying not to wake Kate, she tiptoed out to the hallway.

In the kitchen, she started the coffee and then began to whip up a batch of orange pecan muffins, along with eggs, sausage, and biscuits. Anna had always made her special muffins when guests were present and had passed on the recipe to Ellen to keep the tradition going.

The morning was crisp and clear with a hint of autumn coming. The sun was bright and would soon knock out the slight chill in the air. It was the first week in September and for the first time in years, no one at Haleub Place was heading off to school. This had turned out to be a year for changes and shiftings.

"Good morning, Ellen," a chipper voice spoke behind her.

Quickly, Ellen glanced over her shoulder. "And a good morning to you, too, Walter."

"It's good to have Kate back home. I can see it in your eyes."

"Yes, it is, but I can see that the time of separation was good for both of us. Kate's grown up more than I realized. She's a young woman about to make decisions on her own."

"You say that as if something's about to happen."

"I think it already has."

"What do you mean by that?"

"From the way those two were looking at each other last night, I'd say that Kate and Marcus are more than just good friends."

"I see, and are you okay with that?" he questioned.

"Yes, I think I am. You couldn't ask for a more hard-working, polite, intelligent, young man. I watched them both grow up over the years as good friends. I just never saw the deeper feelings they had for each other."

"It's quite possible that they weren't aware of their feelings either, especially since Marcus has been away at school for the past few years."

"You may be right, Walter. You may be right," she mused as she got the biscuits ready to pop in to the oven. "What's the job for today?"

"A bit more cleaning up of the vegetable garden. The winter squash should be about done, and I need to check on the pumpkins. The apple trees should be about ready to start harvesting as well." He took a sip of coffee. "How about your day?"

"The guests will be here until tomorrow, so I'll be working mostly in the kitchen. If you harvest enough squash, I can fix something for dinner with them. Maybe even muffins or pie."

"That sure is a good incentive to bring them in. Any of those sound wonderful. You're a good cook, Ellen. I can vouch for that," he said, patting his stomach.

Ellen soon had the breakfast tray ready for Anna and Gil, and Walter carried the wonderful aromas down the hall to his room. By the time he got back to the kitchen, Ellen had already taken the serving dishes to the dining room, and Kate had popped into the kitchen.

"Good morning, Mother. I had almost forgotten what it was like to wake up to the smell of orange pecan muffins baking in the oven."

"I tried to be quiet so you could sleep in if you wanted to."

"You didn't wake me up. My stomach did."

"Good morning, Kate," Walter said as he nodded his head toward her. "Did you sleep well?"

"Yes! I sure did. It's good to be home."

A few days later, after the guests were gone, Mr. Jules approached Anna. He found her sitting with Gil on the front porch.

"It's a beautiful day for relaxing—not too hot, not too cold, just right," said Mr. Jules as he sat down in one of the empty chairs.

"Couldn't be finer," replied Gil, smiling peacefully.

"Anna, it's good to see you resting."

"Well, it won't be long before it will be too cold to sit out here, and Gil needs the fresh air," she replied.

"I have a proposition for you, Anna." She looked in Mr. Jules direction, eager to hear what he would say. "Since Kate's graduated, rather than having to go into town to look for employment, what if we let Ellen take over your duties and she can take over her mother's duties? That way, you could have a well-deserved rest and she could stay here with us."

Anna thought about it a minute before she replied. "Only on one condition."

"And what's that?" he asked.

"From time to time, when I feel up to it, I can have access to the kitchen to do a bit of cooking."

"That sounds reasonable enough." He reached over to shake her hand. "Welcome to retirement, Anna. You've worked hard all your life, now it's time to take a rest for yourself."

Gil shifted in his wheelchair. "Anna, it's just a part of life. As we get older, we need to step aside and let the younger ones step up. I'm grateful for Marcus and Walter taking over for me."

"I'm grateful to have Marcus too," added Mr. Jules. "He's a natural in learning the business and the clients like him too."

"Well, I'm grateful to have Ellen and Kate," Anna chimed in. "You couldn't ask for nicer people. They're always ready and willing to pitch in and help out when needed."

"Then that settles it," Mr. Jules said. "We can all relax and let the younger ones take over for us," he chuckled. "This is a beautiful place here, and my father left it in capable hands to carry on. I feel confident that we are all doing the same thing—'leaving it in capable hands.'"

Marcus sat down in the empty chair next to her at the kitchen table. "Kate, how would you like to come with me next Sunday to meet my grandparents? They asked me over for dinner, and I asked them if I could bring a special friend. They said they would be glad to meet you."

She looked up from the letter she was writing to Julia. "Sure, I'd love to. Let me check with Mother to see if there are any guests expected."

"The weekend is free. I already checked before I said yes to them."

"Well, then I guess I'll be going with you," she said, nodding her head. "By the way, did your grandfather ever hear from his brother about your father?"

"Not that I know of. If he did, he didn't mention it to me. Uncle Marshall and I have been trying to find some kind of lead on him, but so far, nothing has turned up."

Kate put her elbows on the table and rested her chin in her hands. "Sometimes I wish I knew more about my father too," she said as she gazed off into space. "I was too young to remember much about him."

Marcus sat there silent for a moment. "Maybe you could write to your grandparents and ask them to tell you about him? Most likely, they would love to share anything they could." He looked straight at Kate, hoping to catch her eye. "It's worth a try; you never know what you might uncover."

Marcus was silent for a few moments and then ventured one more suggestion. "Do you and your mother ever talk about your father?"

"Not really. The subject never comes up."

"Chances are that she wouldn't mind talking about him either, but just doesn't know how to bring the subject up. She could tell you about as far back as when she met him." He sighed and then said something simple but profound. "Your answers may be as close as a question."

Kate sat there quietly, lost in her thoughts, trying to let all this sink in.

"Would you like to go for a walk?" Marcus suggested.

"That sounds good," she said as she picked up her pen and paper. "Let me go put this away and get a sweater. Wait here. I'll be right back."

Marcus waited at the kitchen table until Kate returned. It was almost dusk, and the sun would be setting soon. The house had been fairly quiet today as there were no guests, and Mr. Jules and Marcus had been gone on business most of the day.

Walter gathered several bushel baskets of winter squash from the garden. He then hoisted them up into the wheelbarrow and one at a time wheeled them to the kitchen door. When he had set the last one on the steps, he went in to find Ellen.

Busy fixing lunch, she looked up when he came in.

"I've got some squash for you. Where would you like me to put it?"

"Just set it on the table."

Walter stood there a moment scratching his head as he eyed the table. "Ellen, if you don't mind, perhaps you should come look at it before you decide where you want it."

She wiped her hands on her apron and followed him to the door to look at the squash. "Oh, my goodness!" she exclaimed. "Oh, my goodness!"

Her jaw dropped as she stood there surveying the harvest. There were multiple baskets of pale orange butternut, dark green acorn, and long-stemmed Hubbard squash.

"I didn't bring any of the pumpkins as the vines are still green on most of them. We'll have a bumper crop of those as well."

"Let's open up the cold cellar." She turned and opened a door to the right of the coat stand. Walter had assumed this door was a storage closet of some sort as he had never seen it open before. Ellen pulled the chain to turn on the light, and they went down the short flight of stairs. She pulled another chain to give more light to the twelve-by-twelve-foot room.

Walter quickly surveyed the room, which contained several high benches and one wall with floor-to-ceiling shelves. He saw the remains of last year's potato harvest and the jars of tomatoes and green beans that Ellen had canned from this year's garden.

"This is where we store the garden surplus until we need it. It's close to the kitchen, which makes it very convenient."

"I never knew this was here," Walter said, standing in amazement.

"You can set the baskets on top of the benches, and then when the pumpkins come in, they can go under the benches."

"I'll get right on it, Ellen," he said as he followed her up the stairs. By lunch, he had all the baskets settled in the cellar and the wheelbarrow back to the garden shed.

Chapter 17

Glad that things had settled down at Haleub Place, Lizzy had made arrangements to come for a visit over the weekend. Marcus was waiting for her at the station when her train came in.

"Hello, Mother," he said as he gave her a big hug. "It's good to see you again."

"You too," she said as she returned the hug. "It's been several months, hasn't it? I thought it would be best to let things settle a while before I came for another visit. How is Gil doing?" she inquired as they walked to the car.

"He's gained strength, and Anna is resting and spending time with him. Ellen and Kate are managing the house and the meals quite smoothly, and Walter has the grounds under control. Without this extra work, I've been able to devote more time to learning the business with Uncle Marshall.

"How's that coming along? Do you enjoy it?"

"Yes. I do enjoy it. I go with him whenever he goes to visit clients, and I'm part of the meetings whenever someone comes to Haleub Place on business. When I was younger, I never really thought too much about the business part of our frequent guests. After taking some business courses the last couple of years at school, I have become more interested."

As they approached the car, Marcus opened the door for his mother and then put her bag in the back seat.

"I'm glad you're enjoying your work, son," she said as he slid in the driver's seat. "It makes a big difference that you enjoy what you do for a living."

Marcus started the car and then turned his head to look at his mother.

"Do you enjoy your work?" He put the car in reverse and started backing out.

"Good question." She sighed. "For years, I was just thankful to have a job. It really didn't matter what it was. Having been at the boot factory for so long, I'd made many acquaintances over the years. It wasn't too long after Uncle Marshall found me that I realized I had tunnel vision and was only thinking about myself all the time. I was lonely and bitter about the cards that life had dealt me. I had no vision for the future. I only saw the pain and it held me captive.

After I began making amends to my relationships with you and Mother my eyes were suddenly opened to seeing the lives of others around me at work. I was actually able to make some friends, and that has made work quite pleasant since then."

They both were silent for a few minutes as Marcus turned on to the main road.

"You weren't the only one with tunnel vision. I'm sorry to say that, until today, I don't think I'd ever given a thought about what you did at work. It's nice to know that it's pleasant for you." He glanced out the window. "My tunnel vision has been on school for the last several years. I enjoyed it, but I'm glad that it's behind me."

Lizzy looked over at her son. "I'm glad you had the chance to go to college, Marcus."

"Me too. How's your drawing coming along? Have you had time to keep it up over the summer?"

"Yes. I have. I've taken up something new as well."

"Oh, really? What's that?"

"I've been visiting your grandmother on a regular basis, and she's been giving me cooking lessons. It's been working out pretty well as I have a good excuse for checking up on her more often, and she gets a rest while I do the cooking. We both eat better that way.

"Sounds like a tasty plan," he said, raising his eyebrows.

"Speaking of grandparents, have you heard anything from the Williamses lately?"

"Yes. As a matter of fact, Kate and I are going over there for dinner on Sunday."

"Kate and you?"

"Yes. Kate and me. Since she got back from spending the summer with Julia, we've become a bit more than just friends. Now that we are both out of school, we have more time to spend with each other. Ellen's taken over Anna's duties, and Kate's taken over her mother's duties full time." He looked over at his mother and chuckled. "She's going to be quite a good cook as well."

Lizzy seemed pleased as she looked out her window. She liked Kate and already considered her a part of the family anyway. What better match than someone you'd grown up with? That way there would be no surprises like she'd had with Mitch.

It was almost dinnertime when they arrived. "Oh, that smells so good," Lizzy said as she walked through the front door. Looking over her shoulder to Marcus, she said, "Maybe I can get Ellen to give me a few recipes."

He laughed in reply as he carried her bag to her guest room.

Uncle Marshall stepped into the hall. "I thought I heard voices in here. Lizzy, good to see you again," he said as they gave each other a hug. "How have you been?"

"I'm doing well, very well. And you?"

"Just fine, thank you. How's your mother? Have you seen her lately?"

"Actually, I've been going over there every other weekend to check on her. She's moving a little slower than usual, but other than that she seems to be doing fine. She sends her regards."

Marcus popped in just as they were sitting down in the parlor. With a wink toward his uncle, he asked, "Did Mother tell you about her cooking lessons?"

"No," he said, curiously.

"That's my pretense for my frequent visits to Mother. She gets a rest while I do the cooking. She talks me through each step."

"That sounds like a good idea for both of you. I'm glad you're checking up on her. She never complains about anything so it's hard to know how she's really doing."

"I know. Just last week I noticed how slow she was moving. Her neighbors check up on her on a regular basis and see to it that she gets groceries when she needs them. They're wonderful to her. And Gil, I hear he's doing better."

"Much better," replied her uncle. "We'll go visit him after dinner, and you can see for yourself. I see Ellen coming to let us know its dinnertime."

And with that, they all stood as if on cue, and headed for the dining room table.

"Look who's here," Marshall said as he and Lizzy stood in Gil's doorway.

Anna stood and gave Lizzy a big hug. "It's always good to see you."

"Yes, Lizzy, it's been a while since you've been here," remarked Gil.

"It's good to see you too," she said as she leaned over to give Gil a hug.

"How's your mother doing?" asked Anna.

"She's doing well, moving a bit slower, but doing well. She sends her love to all of you."

"I understand the part about moving slow," Gil said with a nod of his head.

"Me too," Anna chimed in.

"So, how do you like your official retirement, Anna?"

"I'm beginning to like it more than I thought I would. Knowing that everything is resting in the capable hands of Ellen and Kate, makes it a lot easier to let go."

"How fortunate that they have been here for years and already know what to do," Lizzy commented.

"How fortunate for your son, as well," added Marshall with a chuckle.

"What do you mean by that?" Lizzy said as she turned toward her uncle.

"Oh, we all know what's developing between Marcus and Kate," he said with a twinkle in his eye. "What comfort it brings to all of us, knowing that they practically grew up together and have been friends for years."

"Couldn't think of a nicer couple," piped up Gil. "I remember when they first met, how shy Marcus was. It was Jake and Julia that broke the ice for him back then. I think those three were the first friends he ever had."

"You're probably right," Lizzy said lost in thought. "Coming to Haleub Place was the best thing that ever happened to him."

Marshall and Lizzy stayed for a while and then excused themselves. Marcus and Kate had gone for a walk after dinner, which gave Lizzy the perfect opportunity to speak with her uncle alone.

As they settled into the overstuffed chairs in the front room, Lizzy ventured a question. "Uncle Marshall, I'm concerned that if Marcus does find his father, what should my response be? I know he wants to know about his father, but I'm not sure if I want to have any of that stirred up again. Seems like I just put all that to rest too recently to have it opened back up again."

"I understand your concern." He nodded in thought. "It's wise to put some forethought into the matter so you won't be caught off guard if Mitch turns up." He crossed his legs and looked her squarely in the eye. "Do you think you might still have any feelings for him?"

"Any feelings for him right now would include pain. I've let go of all that, thinking that was over. I don't want to go back to the hurt and rejection again."

"Guard your heart, Lizzy," he cautioned. "From what I remember you telling me years ago, it was a gradual thing that led to his final departure. Even though you are still technically married to him, it doesn't mean that he can just walk back into your life without any explanation or accountability on his part.

"Marcus is the one pursuing him, not you. If Mitch is found, let Marcus do the connecting. If Mitch wants to connect with you, let him be the one to make the first move. And remember, you have family to support you. You don't have to do it alone."

Lizzy breathed a sigh of relief. "You're right. This time I *will* surround myself with family. That's what got me into trouble in the first place. I shied away from family and the protection that came with it."

In the morning, Lizzy woke up early and hastened downstairs to the kitchen to find Ellen.

"Good morning, Lizzy. I'm sorry I haven't got breakfast started yet."

"Oh, that was what I was hoping for. I thought maybe I could help out and possibly pick up a recipe or two."

"I'd be glad to share any recipe you want and you are welcome in the kitchen anytime," she said, graciously. Would you like to make the muffins?"

"Orange pecan muffins?" she said, raising her eyebrows hopefully.

"Yes."

"I'd love to, Ellen! Point me in the right direction."

Ellen set out the recipe and all the ingredients. "I'll turn the oven on for you now, so by the time you fill the muffin tins, it'll be the right temperature."

"Thanks, I'll get started right away," she said excitedly. It wasn't long before Lizzy got the muffins in the oven and then began to shred the potatoes while Ellen worked on the eggs and sausage.

"I'm very blessed to find that our children are enjoying each other's company so much. I couldn't think of a finer girl than Kate."

"My mind is very much at ease, knowing Marcus's fine character and that they have been friends for so long. It's good to have peace of mind about your children and those they choose to keep company with."

"Now that I'm a mother, I understand that. I'm sorry to say that when I was his age, my mother had great cause to worry about me. I'm glad that I've had a chance to mend my relationship with my mother and my son. Life can be full of second chances if you take advantage of the opportunity rather than let it pass by."

Marcus and Kate dropped Lizzy off at the station on their way to his grandparents' house.

"It was good seeing you two this weekend," Lizzy said as she hugged them both good-bye."

"You too, Mother. When are you going to invite us up for some of your home cooking?" he said teasingly.

"Good question, I'll let you know…soon, I hope. Say hello to the Williamses for me. I'd like to meet them someday, that is, if they want to meet me."

They waved as she boarded the train and then set off for Hamilton.

"I'm glad you're coming with me, Kate," he said as he glanced over at her. "It's so nice to have somebody to share all this with. Sometimes, when you meet people, you just want to share them with others you know."

"I know what you mean. I wish you could meet Jake and Julia's grandparents some time."

"I'd like that, perhaps I will."

The drive went by quickly, and before they knew it, they were in Hamilton. Marcus parked the car and they walked up the sidewalk. Before they even had a chance to knock, the door opened wide.

Marcus's grandmother was overjoyed. She gave Marcus a big hug. "It's good to see you again. And this must be Kate," she said as she reached to hug her as well.

"It's nice to meet you, Mrs. Williams," Kate said politely as they stepped inside the house.

Mr. Williams met them in the hallway as he came around the corner. "Good to have you both," he said as he threw an arm around each of them. "Come in the living room and have a seat," he said as he pointed the way with his hand.

"We enjoyed the drive over here. It was beautiful with all the leaves beginning to change colors," Kate said.

"I think the heat of the summer is finally behind us. My garden is about done, except for a few pumpkins," Mr. Williams explained.

"We had a plentiful harvest as well." Marcus agreed. "An abundance of winter squash and pumpkins too."

"We're glad you came, Kate. It's nice to meet you," Mr. Williams said.

"You too, Mr. Williams," she said with a smile that made her eyes sparkle.

Kate could easily light up a room. She was even tempered and still had that zeal for life that she had displayed as a child, always ready for fun. As they talked, she took note of the pictures hanging on the wall, assuming the child was Marcus's father.

Soon, the dinner was ready and on the table, and Mrs. Williams was calling them all to come sit down in the dining room.

"Everything's hot. Help yourself," she said as she took her seat.

They passed the serving dishes around until everyone's plate was full.

"This looks and smells delicious, Grandmother."

"Mmm," was all Kate said as she took her first bite.

"Have you heard anything from your brother lately?" Marcus asked between mouthfuls.

"No, I haven't heard a thing since I wrote to him several weeks ago. I suppose, depending on where he is, that it takes a while to forward something to him. Have you and your uncle uncovered anything?"

"Nothing, so far. We think we have a connection and then at the last minute, it falls through. Every avenue we've followed so far has come up empty. Uncle Marshall said that finding my mother was so much easier than searching for my father." Marcus paused for a moment. "Speaking of my mother, she sends her regards and would be interested in meeting you sometime if you'd like. She wasn't sure how you would feel about meeting her."

"Hmph," was his grandfather's only reply. His grandmother looked to her husband, but refrained from saying anything.

Marcus was learning that his grandfather didn't take to new things very readily. He needed time to think about them and let them settle a while before he was ready to move forward on anything. He was prepared to not have an answer for his mother quite yet. Most likely, they would agree to meet her but would probably need some time to get used to the idea first.

Chapter 18

"What a beautiful, crisp autumn morning," remarked Marshall at the breakfast table. "Did you sleep well, Marcus?"

"Yes, I did. Autumn is one of my favorite seasons of the year. Even though the growing season is ending, it always feels as if something new is about to happen. Perhaps it reminds me of starting a new year at school."

September was almost over and the leaves of the trees were displaying vibrant yellows, autumn golds, shades of deep orange, and brilliant reds. It was a magical time of the year where fallen leaves produced a crunching sound that almost echoed with each footstep. The pumpkins were ripe, the apple harvest was in and the vegetable garden was put to rest until next spring.

"As soon as we finish breakfast, we should probably get on the road to Chestertown. Mr. Snyder is expecting us by late morning and is treating us to lunch as well."

"Nothing like going from one meal to another," Marcus said, grinning.

The scenery was beautiful along the way as they drove past the fall trees in their prime. Marshall briefed Marcus on the business at hand so it would be fresh in his mind when they arrived.

Mr. Snyder's office was nestled in the business district of the bustling town. Three stories high, the brown brick building shared walls with those on either side of it. The row of buildings filled the entire block, some similar in brick or stone, but each with its own unique architecture and trim.

Marcus pulled around to the back lot to park, and they walked up the wide white stone steps at the back entrance. Marshall pushed the bell, and within seconds the door opened.

"Come in, Mr. Jules, come in!" the tall, blonde, middle-aged woman said politely. "And who is with you today?" she said as she closed the door behind them.

Mr. Jules extended his arm, greeting her with a handshake.

"Mrs. Lindsey, this is my nephew, Marcus Williams."

Marcus greeted her with a handshake as well. "It's nice to meet you, Mrs. Lindsey."

"It's good to meet you too, Marcus." She turned to walk down the hall. "Right this way, gentlemen. Mr. Snyder has been expecting you."

Together, they walked down the wide hallway following the secretary. As their footsteps echoed on the polished wooden floor, Marcus observed the tall ceilings and the various paintings hung on either side of the pale yellow walls.

"What a beautiful collection of paintings," Marcus remarked out loud.

With a turn of her head, Mrs. Lindsey spoke over her shoulder. "Mr. Snyder is quite a lover of fine art." She knocked three short raps on the door at the end of the hallway.

"Come in," said a deep voice on the other side of the door. "Ah, Marshall," he said as his secretary opened the wide door. A tall, dark-haired gentleman stood up from behind a large oak desk. His serious look broke into a smile as they entered the room. "This must be your nephew, Marcus. Pleased to meet you," he said as he shook hands with both of them.

"Good to see you again, Samuel," said Marshall. "It's been too long since our last meeting."

Mrs. Lindsey quietly excused herself and left the room, softly closing the door behind her.

"Have a seat, gentlemen," Mr. Snyder said as he sat down and motioned toward the two leather armchairs in front of his desk. "Before we get down to business, I have some information for you," he said as he handed a piece of paper to Mr. Jules.

Accustomed to Mr. Snyder's abrupt nature, Marshall pulled out his glasses and glanced at the paper. "Hmmm, I see," was his only response. "Thank you very much, Samuel. I'm most grateful for this." He folded it up and placed it in an inner pocket of his suit jacket.

They quickly got down to business and before they knew it, two hours had quickly passed. As the clock struck one, Mr. Snyder looked up and said, "Let's break for lunch, gentlemen. We have a luncheon reservation for 1:15 p.m. at Morse Haven. It's a short walk, a block away." As Mr. Snyder stood up, he said, "We'll finish this up after lunch."

Marcus was grateful for the break as the business meeting had been quite intense up till now. He had been silent during much of it, only joining in when addressed directly. As they stepped outside, the air still had that touch of fall crispness lingering from the morning. Falling behind a couple steps, Marcus let his uncle and Mr. Snyder walk together down the sidewalk. Chestertown was an old established city, larger than any he had visited before. He was fascinated by the architecture of the buildings surrounding them.

"Good day, Mr. Snyder," the host said as they stepped into the restaurant. "Your table is ready. Step this way, please." They followed him to a table nestled back in a corner, already set for three.

Marcus excused himself for a moment to visit the men's room. He breathed a sigh of relief and shook his head a few times. *I can do this. I can make it through lunch. I can make it through the afternoon.* He took another deep breath and then returned to the table.

His uncle caught his eye as he was about to sit down and gave him a reassuring look.

"I've already ordered today's special for all of us. No need to look at a menu," Mr. Snyder said matter-of-factly and then fired a question at him. "Tell me about yourself, Marcus."

"Well, sir," Marcus started slowly so as not to stammer. "I just graduated from Kings College a few months ago with a major in business. My uncle offered to teach me the family business, and that's what I've been working on for the past few months."

"Do you have any vision for your future?" His eyes seemed to be staring deep into his soul.

"It's a dream to be where I am today, a college graduate with a future in the family business."

"Is that all you've got? Are you just going to carry on someone else's vision, or do you have one for yourself?"

Not knowing what else to say, Marcus was silent a moment. A quick glance at his uncle let him know that he was on his own on this one.

"Thank you for asking. Those are very good questions that I need to know the answer to. I do have dreams, but now that I think about it, they are not near big enough."

"Well, let's see what you've got to start with. Lay it out for me."

"Okay, here's what I've got. I'd like to find my father if possible, I'd like to marry a certain girl, I'd like to learn this business well enough to carry on for my uncle, and I'd like to keep Haleub Place going so it could continue to be a place of restoration, peace, and beauty." He felt like he'd been wrung out and his life and dreams had been reduced to the size of a nutshell.

A waiter brought their drinks and set them on the table along with a basket of fresh rolls. It was a welcome momentary diversion. As harsh as this line of questioning had been, Marcus was actually grateful for the honesty it unveiled. Nothing like getting to the point in a hurry.

They sipped their drinks and passed the hot rolls, dark rye with a crusty top covered with various seeds.

"These are delicious," Marshall said as he swallowed his last bite. He reached for another and then passed the basket around. "How is your wife doing, Samuel?"

"She's doing fine. There are several groups around town that she has become quite involved in and that keeps her going."

"You'll have to bring her to Haleub Place sometime for a visit," encouraged Marshall.

"Perhaps I will. Thank you for your kind invitation."

Marcus shuddered just thinking about it. *That could prove to be an intense visit.*

Their food soon arrived, and Marcus was beginning to think that his inquisition was over. The special of the day was hearty beef stew, and the waiter brought more hot rolls and a plate with a wedge of cheese the size of a slice of pie.

Looking up from his large bowl of stew, Marcus remarked, "This is the best stew that I've ever eaten."

Mr. Snyder reached for his napkin to wipe his moustache. "That's what I like about this place. When they say it's the special of the day, their emphasis is on the fact that it is one of their 'specialties.'"

Their waiter came to start clearing their table. "Will anyone be having dessert today?"

"Do you have any specials today?" asked Marshall, glancing at Mr. Snyder.

"Yes, our special today is apple walnut cobbler."

"Bring us all one of those, please," Mr. Snyder spoke up. Turning his attention back to Marcus, he locked his eyes with Marcus. "You've got a good start. It's important to know your past, where you've come from, in order to know what you're made of."

Marcus nodded and blinked, hesitant to look away from those intense eyes.

"It's good to know your weaknesses and strengths up front. You can use them to your advantage and know those things to run with and those things to steer clear of." He paused a moment to let that sink in and then continued. "It's good to know your passions and pursue those things that will bring joy to you and others as well."

As Mr. Snyder sat there a moment with a look of satisfaction on his face, Marcus began to relax a bit. Marshall sat silent with an amused look on his face. He had known ahead of time that there was no way to really prepare Marcus for this meeting. Mr. Snyder was blunt and abrupt but had an uncanny ability to read someone's character. If taken to heart, his wisdom and insight could prove to be quite helpful.

Marcus looked away for a minute and reached for his glass to take a drink of water. As he set his glass down, Mr. Snyder continued.

"It's good to recognize and use your skills for what they were designed for and not covet someone else's. You've got a good foundation to start with, Marcus. Build on it. Make it your own. Consider the cost before you start. Your passions and skills are only designed to fuel *your* dreams, not someone else's. Don't be afraid to ask directions on the journey. Know where you're going. If you get lost, go back to where you made a wrong turn and ask directions."

"Thank you, sir," replied Marcus. "You've given me a lot to think about. You are a very wise man."

"As is your uncle," he returned, glancing at Marshall. "You're in good hands, son. I believe you will make your mark."

The waiter arrived carrying a tray with their dessert.

"Three apple walnut cobblers," he said as he placed them on the table one by one. "Will there be anything else today?"

"No, thank you. You can bring the bill to me," Mr. Snyder said.

"I hope you enjoy your dessert," the waiter said as he refilled their glasses and then left to figure the bill.

"This is marvelous," said Marshall as he took his first bite.

"Mmmm," was all Marcus said as he dug in for a second bite.

Mr. Snyder picked up his fork and dug into his as well.

The waiter brought the bill as they were finishing up their dessert.

"Everything was delicious!" Marshall said, addressing the waiter.

"Yes, I agree," added Marcus.

"Nothing but the best, as usual," said Mr. Snyder as he reached in his pocket and pulled out enough cash to cover their meal. "Keep the change," he said. "Fine service!" And with that, he rose from the table, and they all filed out of the restaurant, very satisfied customers.

It was a short walk back to the office, and they picked up where they had left off before lunch. Marcus was silent for the remainder of the afternoon, intent on listening to every word that was said as well as pondering all that had been said during lunch. Two hours quickly passed before the meeting came to a close.

Mr. Snyder rose from his chair and stretched out his hand to Marcus. "It was good to meet you, Marcus," he said with a firm handshake.

"You too, sir. I look forward to our next meeting."

Marshall reached out his hand. "It's always good to see you, Samuel. Maybe next time you can come to Haleub Place and bring your wife."

"Yes, she would like that. Perhaps we will. Have a good trip home." He nodded.

Marshall and Marcus stopped by Mrs. Lindsey's desk to say good-bye and then let themselves out of the building. The bright sun had warmed things up enough to knock the morning chill out of the air. As Marcus started the car and began backing out of the parking space, Marshall looked over at him and caught his eye.

"You handled yourself very well, Marcus. There's really no way to prepare someone for a meeting with

Mr. Snyder. You never know what he might say. Some are put off by his abruptness, and others glean from it as you did."

"I respect that man and what he says," Marcus replied. "He speaks the truth and gets right to the point. He asks good questions, very thought-provoking questions."

"That he does," agreed Marshall.

The drive home was pleasant enough. They enjoyed the fall scenery as they reviewed the day's business. Marcus was beginning to understand more and more, that a huge part of business had as much to do with people skills as it had to do with technical knowledge. Each client was a unique individual, and a good businessman understood and appreciated them for who they were.

After dinner that evening, Kate and Marcus went for a walk.

"Kate, I met a man today that asked me a lot of questions that really made me think."

"About the business?" she asked.

"Well, yes and no. He asked me what my dreams were and that includes my future in the business. It gave me a lot to think about and sort out in my mind." He hesitated a minute and then asked, "Kate, do you know what your dreams are?"

"No one has ever asked me that before. Good question." She thought for a moment. "My goal was to graduate from high school, find a job, and maybe someday get married. I don't know that I ever thought beyond that."

"That was sort of my answer too. Graduate from college, carry on the business and Haleub Place, and settle down with someone." He took a deep breath before he continued. "Mr. Snyder encouraged me to discover my past in order to pursue my future with my eyes wide open to my strengths, as well as my weaknesses. If I can identify the pitfalls of the past, it may be that I can stop myself from falling into them." He looked over at Kate. "That's why I want to know about my father, what he was like, what happened to make him just disappear. Since you've met my grandparents, maybe you can help me put together some of the pieces of this puzzle.

"I'm so glad you're here, Kate," he said as he pulled her close with his arm around her shoulders.

She rested her head on his shoulder. "I'm glad you're here too, Marcus."

Chapter 19

"Could you stop by the study after breakfast?" Marshall asked as they were eating at the dining room table. "I've got something that I'd like to show you."

"Sure. Any business trips coming up soon?" Marcus asked.

"Well, the Bloomfields are coming here tomorrow to stay for a few days, so it may be next week before we'll be going anywhere." He picked up his napkin to wipe his mouth and then refolded it and slipped it into the napkin ring lying by his plate. "If you'll excuse me, Marcus, I've got to go check on something. I'll see you in a few minutes."

Marcus finished his breakfast and gathered his dishes to take in to the kitchen. "Good morning, Kate," he said as he set his dishes down by the sink. "It looks like I'll be home today, so I'll check in with you later as the day goes by."

"Mother and I will be getting ready for the guests coming tomorrow."

"Yes, I heard. I guess I'll be getting ready for the business end of the stay. I'll see you later," he said as he excused himself and headed to his uncle's study.

"Knock, knock," he said as he walked in the room.

"Have a seat," his uncle said as he gestured toward one of the chairs in front of his desk. He unfolded a sheet of paper and laid it on the edge of his desk in front of Marcus. "Take a look at this."

Marcus picked it up and read the handwritten name and address. He looked over at his uncle. "Where did you get this?" he asked in amazement.

"Mr. Snyder handed it to me when we were in his office. You'd had enough thrown at you from his hard questions, so I waited until morning to give this to you."

He looked back at the paper and read it again. "He only lives about four hours away; I'm going to see him."

"Would you like some company, or would you prefer to go by yourself?"

"Thanks for your offer, but this is something I need to do on my own." He sat there in a daze for a minute as he tried to think this through. "If I leave right now, I can be there and back before the Bloomfields arrive tomorrow."

"Take your time if you need to. The Bloomfields will be here for a few days, and we can wait to discuss business until you get back," his uncle assured him.

"I'll go get a few things together, just in case I end up spending the night somewhere along the way." He excused himself and went to find Kate to tell her the news. Within a half an hour, Marcus was on the road to go find his father.

As he drove along the highway, he felt like he was on a journey going back in time. Grateful for the long drive, Marcus began to plan out in his mind what he would say to his father. He thought back to the day he had met his grandfather at the repair shop. That awkwardness he had felt then would most likely be multiplied in intensity when he finally came face to face with his father.

An hour had passed when he found himself thinking about Mr. Snyder. *I wonder if that was why he was asking me such hard questions. He knew I was about to connect with my father and was trying to prepare me ahead of time. I'm glad Uncle Marshall waited till morning.*

The closer Marcus got to Southbridge, the more his stomach began to turn and tighten in knots. As soon as he passed the "Welcome to Southbridge" sign, he began looking for a place to pull over. Spotting a gas station up ahead, he turned in and got out to ask directions. Marcus motioned to the attendant as he pulled the paper with the address on it out of his pocket.

"Could you direct me to Huntington Way?" he asked as he approached the tall gentleman.

"You're not far from it," he answered. Pointing straight ahead, he continued, "Take the third road on the right. Follow it to the bottom of the hill and Huntington Way will be on your left."

"Thank you very much, sir. You've been most helpful." As Marcus started to turn to head back to his car, the attendant stood still as if he wanted to say something more.

"Excuse me," he said, causing Marcus to turn his head. "I don't mean to pry, but Huntington Way is in a residential neighborhood and has very few houses on it. Are you looking for someone in particular?"

Turning back to face the man, Marcus swallowed hard and looked him straight in the eye. "I'm looking for Mitchell Troy Williams."

The attendant, looking visibly shaken, replied, "I'm Mitchell Troy Williams." Looking hard at Marcus, he asked, "What do you want from me?"

Marcus glanced at his watch. "I'd like to ask you a few questions. Do you have a break anytime soon where we could talk for a few minutes?"

"My lunch break is in about fifteen minutes. We can talk over there," he said, pointing to two picnic tables sitting under a maple tree.

Two cars pulled into the station, and Mitch quickly turned his attention to the customers. Grateful for the interruption, Marcus headed inside to get something to eat.

He studied the menu for a minute and then ordered. "Two club sandwiches and two large apple ciders, please."

The order was ready in a few minutes. He paid for it and carried it outside to the table. The autumn leaves on the tree gave a brilliant glow to the eating area. He felt like he was bathed in light as he sat down to collect his thoughts.

This was the moment he had been waiting for. He watched as his father finished up with the last customer and another attendant arrived to cover his lunch break. He went in to wash his hands and then joined Marcus at the table.

Marcus handed him a drink and a sandwich. "I hope you like the club," he said, referring to the sandwich.

"Yes, thanks," he replied as he took a bite.

Marcus took a drink and then cleared his throat. "Would your parents happen to be James and Evelyn Williams from Hamilton?"

"Yes," he answered cautiously. "Is everything all right with them? Are they well?"

"They're fine," assured Marcus. "I just wanted to make sure I had the right person before I went any further. My name is Marcus Reston Williams. My mother's name is Lizzy Hopkins Williams." At this, Mitch stared at him in disbelief.

Marcus paused for a moment to let this sink in before he continued. "Shortly after you left, she discovered that she was pregnant and had no way of letting you know. I'm the one that's looking for you, not her."

Mitch finally found his voice and managed to stammer, "Then, you…are my son?" he said in disbelief. How can that be? How did you find me?"

"It wasn't easy. You didn't leave much of a trail to follow."

"This is all such a shock to me. I don't even know what to say. You mentioned my parents. Do you know them?"

"I just met them this summer. In my search for you, I ran across their address and sent them a letter explaining who I was. I hoped that they would be a connection for me to find you. They are doing well but still bewildered and hurt, not knowing what happened to you."

"Where do you live, Marcus?"

"I live with my uncle at Haleub Place, about four hours away."

"Why did you want to find me? I'm sure your mother didn't have many good things to say about me after I left."

"Actually, she didn't have much to say about you at all until I started asking questions recently. Something deep down inside of me wanted to know what you were like. I wanted to know where I came from, what I was made of. I've enjoyed getting to know your parents. Your mother is such a sweet, loving lady, and your father is reserved but loosening up a bit."

"I don't know what to say, Marcus," he said, looking ashamed of himself.

They were quiet for a few minutes as they ate their sandwiches. Marcus took a big drink of his cider and then gathered the courage to ask the question he'd wondered about for years.

Once again, he looked his father in the eye and asked, "What made you leave? Why did you go?"

"Your mother, Lizzy, deserved someone better than me. I had caught her in a time of weakness and took advantage of her."

"What do you mean by that?" ventured Marcus.

"Her father had died not long before I met her, and she was looking for someone to fill a void in her life. She latched on to the first older male that paid attention to her. An easy catch for me, a disaster for her."

Mitch looked up from the table and glanced at Marcus who was staring intensely at him, taking it all in.

"Now you know the truth. I wasn't man enough to stay. I probably would have been a horrible father to you. You probably wish that you had never found me now. You could have imagined me any way you wanted, but now you know the ugly truth. He's sitting right across from you." And with that he looked back down at the table in silence.

Not knowing how to respond, Marcus was silent as well. He took another bite of his lunch and thought for a moment as he chewed.

In the awkwardness of the moment, Mitch reached for his sandwich, grateful to have something to do with his hands. He finished his last bite and started to get up.

Marcus struggled to find his voice.

"Wait…thank you for being honest with me and telling me the truth. You didn't have to. You could have made up anything you wanted me to believe, but you didn't."

"I guess I'd better let you get back to work. Your lunch break is probably about over. Here is my card," he said as he reached into his wallet and pulled out a business card his uncle had made for him.

"Thank you. Thank you for coming."

Marcus looked over at the cars lined up at the station. "I'll take the tray inside. It was nice to meet you," he said as they parted with a handshake.

After taking the tray back inside the shop, Marcus got back into his car and let out a big sigh of relief. He backed out of the parking space and headed back the way he had come in, waving to his father as he drove out of the station.

The search was over, and he knew the easy part was behind him. The hard part was just beginning. He had made the initial contact and his father would probably need some time to sort all this out.

It was dark by the time Marcus pulled in at Haleub Place. With the sun down and a small breeze stirring, there was a definite chill in the air. After taking his things to his room, he stopped by his uncle's study.

"Knock, knock," he said as he entered the open door of the study. Startled, Marshall turned around in his chair. "I didn't expect you back so soon. How did it go?"

Marcus sat down in one of the chairs in front of his uncle's desk. "Perfect timing. He just happened to be working at the gas station where I stopped to ask directions and was about to go on his lunch break when I arrived. We only had a short time to talk over lunch before he had to get back to work. I left my card with him. He has a lot to think about right now."

"You're right, he does. You probably stirred up a lot of things he's had buried for a long time. Did you ask him why he left?"

"Yes, I did. He said my mother deserved better than him, and frankly, if that's the way he felt about it, maybe she did." He sat there for a moment, lost in thought, before he said good night and headed for his room.

Alone in his room, he sat down at his desk to compose a letter. On the long drive home, Marcus had played over and over in his mind, the short meeting he had had with his father. After the initial shock of meeting him face to face had passed, he began to think of things he'd wished he said.

Dear Dad… He struck through that and began again. *Dear Father…* That didn't seem right either. After much thought, he started again.

Dear Mitch,

I know our meeting today was quite a shock to you, suddenly finding out that you had a grown son. Perhaps I should have written a letter to you first, before just showing up.

As you can imagine, I have wondered about who my father was, for a long time. I will leave it up to you as to whether or not you want to have any further contact with me. I would be open to that, but don't want to impose myself on you any further if the feeling is not mutual.

I want to thank you again for being honest with me about why you left. This letter is not meant to bring any condemnation on you in any way for doing what you did. Sometimes we do things we feel we need to do and then try to move on.

At one point, while growing up, my mother left me with another family thinking I would be better off without her. That family abandoned me as well and I felt very alone.

It wasn't until some others took me in and were consistently patient and kind with me, that I began to trust anyone again.

My mother and I have worked through forgiveness of many hurts of the past and over time, have come to have a healthy relationship with each other. It is my desire to offer you forgiveness and a new start as well. I forgive you for not being there for me or my mother. There's nothing we can do now to change the past, but we do have a chance to change the future.

It's never too late to start over. You can take steps to mend the brokenness in your life.

Thank you again for meeting with me today and giving me the chance to talk with you. I sincerely appreciate it.

Marcus

Chapter 20

"Good morning, Ellen," Walter said as he came through the back door of the kitchen. "It's a bit chilly outside this morning."

"Good morning to you, Walter," she said with a smile.

"What's the job for today?"

"There are guests coming this afternoon: a father, mother, and two young children. Kate and I will be getting things ready for them."

"What's your job for today?"

"I believe this is pumpkin day. With the weather changing so fast, I think it's time to bring them all to the cold cellar."

Ellen started chuckling. "If there are as many pumpkins as there were winter squash, it might take all morning or longer to get them in."

"Get what in?" said Kate as she walked into the kitchen.

"The pumpkins."

"I'll ask Marcus if he can lend a hand," she said. "I'm sure he wouldn't mind a bit. I've seen those pumpkins. Some of them are large enough to fill a wheelbarrow."

"Thank you, Kate," said Walter." I would be glad for the help if he's not busy."

Ellen suggested, "Maybe I could make pumpkin pie for dinner, pumpkin muffins for lunch, pumpkin pancakes for breakfast, pumpkin bread for tea…"

"I guess we'll all be enjoying pumpkins soon enough." Kate laughed. "Maybe you could send a few recipes, along with a pumpkin or two, to Lizzy for her next cooking adventure."

Laughing, Ellen looked up and said, "Be on the lookout for who we can bless with pumpkins."

Walter took the breakfast tray down to Gil and Anna. Kate volunteered to take the breakfast to the dining room so she could ask Marcus about helping Walter. By the time she returned to the kitchen, Walter had sat down to eat breakfast himself.

"Marcus said he'd be glad to help you out this morning after breakfast, Walter. Mother, I'll take care of the guest rooms and the house if you want to get started on the cooking."

"That sounds good," said Ellen as she sat down to join them at the kitchen table for breakfast.

Marcus and Walter started with the largest pumpkins first, that way if it took longer than the morning, Walter could finish easily by himself. It felt good to be working in the cool crisp morning. Before too long, all the leaves would be on the ground and the gardens would be put to rest for another winter. Walter had been making mental notes over the past few months of all the dead limbs and fallen branches to cut up for firewood. Winter was just around the corner, and he wanted to make sure there was enough firewood for the winter.

"I'm sorry I can't stay to help you get the job finished," Marcus said as he surveyed the remaining pumpkins in the field. "At least the largest ones are already done. I've got to meet with Uncle Marshall before the guests arrive this afternoon."

"Thanks for your help, Marcus. It would have been a real challenge to get these larger ones in by myself. It'll be no problem getting the rest in by this afternoon."

Marcus stopped in the kitchen to get a drink before going to his uncle's study.

"Knock, knock," he said as he entered the study. "When you get a chance, take a look at the cold cellar. We have an abundance of winter squash and pumpkins, and Walter's not finished bringing the smaller ones in."

"So there will be pies soon?" his uncle asked expectantly.

"There was talk of one perhaps by dinner tonight. We'll see," said Marcus hopefully.

"Now, tell me about your visit with your father yesterday."

Marcus settled in the armchair in front of the desk.

"Well," he began. "He was working as an attendant at a service station, and I offered to buy him lunch, which I got from the shop in the station. When he came to join me at an outside table, I told him who I was. He wanted to know why I was looking for him and how I found him.

"I left my card in case he wanted to make contact. He probably needs some time to process everything.

"You are to be commended, Marcus. You did a fine job of reaching out. Are you going to tell your mother or your grandparents?"

"I'm not sure. I think he deserves a chance to contact them on his own if he wants to. I'll give him some time to think things through, maybe a few weeks, and then go from there."

"That seems like a fair plan," commented his uncle.

"He was very honest about why he left, which shows that he has given it some thought somewhere along the way."

"Why did he leave?"

"Selfishness."

"Well, I'm glad that mystery is solved. The rest is up to him," he said as he collected some papers on his desk. "Here are some things I put together for you to look over before the Bloomfields arrive."

The rest of the day was a blur for Mitch as he went through the motions at work. When the day was over, he went home and sat in a daze in his armchair in his living room. He was not proud of what he'd become, even though he had a job and a roof over his head, the truth was, he was pretty miserable. He was not really living, only existing day to day. Except for a few acquaintances at work, he had no friends. His former good looks had been replaced with a furrowed brow and a scowl on his face. His shoulders had become hunched, and he walked with a slow gait, never in a hurry to get anywhere.

It took a lot of guts for Marcus to come looking for me, especially after the way I deserted his mother. I guess the least I could do is to let my parents know that I'm okay so they will stop worrying about me. It never occurred to me that they would even care after the way I treated them.

Mitch pulled Marcus's card out of his pocket and read his name out loud. "Marcus Reston Williams." He sat there dumbfounded. *I have a son...*

He glanced out the window and saw that it was dark already. With great effort, he made himself get up and fix a sandwich for dinner. The events of the day had taken a toll on him, and he was ready to lie down and go to sleep.

The Bloomfields arrived not long after lunch. Ellen greeted them at the front door.

"Welcome to Haleub Place! Come in, come in!"

"I'm Preston, and this is my wife, Sandy."

"Pleased to meet you both. You can call me Ellen. And who are these fine boys hiding behind you?"

"This is Derrick," Sandy, said pointing to her blue-eyed, black-haired son. "And this is our two-year-old, Dakota." He had a grin from ear to ear beneath his curly red hair and brown eyes.

Just then, Mr. Jules and Marcus appeared around the corner and stepped into the hallway.

"I thought I heard voices. It's nice to meet your family, Preston. You must be Sandy," he said, reaching out to shake her hand. "Good to see you again," he said as he greeted Preston with a handshake as well. "This is my nephew, Marcus Williams."

"It's nice to meet you all," Marcus said, as he shook hands in greeting.

"Let's all sit down in here," Marshall said as he led the way to the front room.

Ellen excused herself and headed to the kitchen to get a tray ready with refreshments. She filled up four large mugs and two smaller cups of cold apple cider and then set a large basket of fresh baked pumpkin muffins on the tray. They had just sat down, when she brought in the tray and set it down at a table in the corner of the room. The young boys wasted no time in checking out the goodies and were at her side in an instant.

"Boys," their mother said, getting up quickly. "You need to sit down while you eat." She glanced around the room and spotted a small table with two chairs. "Come over here," she said as she set out their cups of cider and two plates with a muffin on them.

Ellen winked at the boys as she left the room. She had a feeling that the next few days could prove to be quite amusing.

"Phew!" Walter said as he hung up his coat and hat in the back room. "They're all in."

Ellen poured a tall mug of cold apple cider and set it down on the table.

"Here," she said as she set out a few muffins. "Take a break and try out the pumpkin muffins."

Walter sat down and took a bite. "I vote yes on these, and there's no shortage of pumpkins."

"Walter," she said, chuckling, "you vote yes on everything I cook."

"That's because it's all good," he said, patting his stomach. "The next time you ladies go downstairs to the cold cellar, be very careful where you step. There are pumpkins everywhere."

"I want to go see," said Kate as she stopped peeling potatoes and wiped her hands on her apron.

"I might as well go too," Ellen said, following her.

Kate pulled the chain to turn on the light. "Oh my goodness!" she said in amazement as she slowly went down the steps. "I don't ever remember there being this many pumpkins before." She pulled the chain to turn on the second light.

Ellen stopped at the bottom of the stairs, speechless as she surveyed the room. "He wasn't kidding, was he, Kate?" she said softly.

They turned off the lights as they came back up the stairs and shut the door.

"I hope you like pumpkin," Ellen said to Walter as she passed by him at the table.

"I like anything you cook, Ellen."

She smiled at him and then got back to work preparing dinner. Kate watched and listened as her mother and Walter bantered back and forth with friendly chatter. She could see that they were good for each other. This may be just what her mother needed to fill the gap since she had been away all summer and was spending more and more of her free time with Marcus.

He had a gentle nature, always willing to pitch in and help when he could. Gil and Anna enjoyed his company and rested in the fact that the grounds were in very capable hands. Walter honored Gil by asking his advice and keeping him posted on how things were growing. He even wheeled him around the grounds a few times in his wheelchair to show him what he'd done. It was peaceful here, and those who came here took on that same nature—it was transforming.

"If you'd like to take the boys outside, there's plenty of room to run," said Mr. Jules. "Except for the mums, most of the gardens are finished blooming. A few of the trees still have some autumn color on them. Perhaps your boys would enjoy jumping in a leaf pile."

At this suggestion, Derrick looked at his mother and father expectantly. Sandy looked at her husband and then jumped at the opportunity.

"That sounds like a wonderful idea, especially since they've been cooped up in the car all morning."

"I'll let Marcus show you to your room first, and then we can all meet on the front porch in a few minutes."

Marcus helped Mr. Bloomfield carry their luggage to the room and then excused himself to go get a jacket before meeting them outside. Mr. Jules had gone to get a jacket as well and was waiting for them on the porch.

He led them around to the back and showed them where the maze was while Marcus went to go get a rake for the leaves. The boys squealed with delight as they raced back and forth between the hedges.

"You have a beautiful place," remarked Sandy, "even in the fall."

"Thank you. Our groundskeeper does a wonderful job keeping up with the flowers, the orchard, the vegetable garden, and everything else. In fact, those pumpkin muffins we just ate are made from pumpkins just harvested this morning."

"From the taste of those muffins, I'd venture to say that you have a wonderful cook as well."

"That we do. No doubt about that," Mr. Jules heartily agreed.

It wasn't long before Marcus called out, "The leaf pile is ready. Come and get it!"

Preston, who had been enjoying the maze almost as much as the boys, managed to corral them in the direction of the leaf pile. As soon as Derrick spotted the pile, he took off running and was the first to jump in. Dakota was close behind him but not able to jump very high, so he just plowed into the leaf pile with all his might.

There was a great fluttering of leaves amidst little voices shouting, "Look, look at me!" followed by squeals of laughter. The boys' laughter was contagious and soon had everyone laughing with them.

Standing there, leaning on the rake, Marcus saw a snapshot picture of what he and Kate might be like in a few years; two boys of their own, perhaps, jumping in leaf piles. Without a doubt, he knew that Kate was the one for him. He'd known her almost half of his life and they had been friends for just as long.

"Marcus," his uncle's voice shook him out of his day-dream, "we need another leaf pile."

"Sure thing, sorry," he said as he started raking up the pile again.

Mr. Jules and Sandy sat down on a nearby bench as the excitement continued over at the leaf pile. The boys even convinced their father and Marcus to jump in with them. This was just the release Marcus needed after the emotional wrenching he'd been through the day before. The fun and laughter was a source of renewed strength pouring back into him what had been poured out. As fast as he could rake the leaves into a pile, the boys jumped back in, never seeming to tire.

"Thanks, Marcus," the boys' father said as he reached for the rake. "I'll take a turn at raking while you take a little rest.

"You're fortunate that the leaves are still on the ground. Any other day they would probably be already raked up and out of the way, but instead, we were bring-ing in the pumpkins this morning." Marcus added. "It's a win/win situation. We get pumpkin muffins to eat and leaf piles to jump in."

"What a great place to live. Did you grow up here?"

"I've lived here since I was twelve. It is a pretty awesome place to live."

"I'm sure Derrick and Dakota will want to come out to the maze and the leaf pile tomorrow. Any chance you could hold off raking the leaves while they're here?"

"Sure, I'll ask Mr. Wagner not to rake in this area for the next couple of days."

The boys seemed to have boundless energy and only stopped when their parents told them it was time to go in and get cleaned up for dinner.

"One good thing about the boys playing," their mother shared with Mr. Jules, "when they play, they play hard. And when they play hard, they sleep soundly at night."

The conversation was quite lively at the dinner table that night.

"Why do the leaves fall off the trees?" asked Derrick.

All the adults looked up to see who would be the one to answer. After an awkward silence, Mr. Jules spoke up.

"Every year in the spring, a tree makes new green leaves to give shade to the earth when it gets hot in the summer. Once the weather starts getting cooler, the green changes to yellow, orange, red, or brown. The leaves hold on as long as they can, but after a while they get tired and finally let go and fall to the ground. That gives little boys like you the chance to run and jump in them."

At this, Derrick giggled and took another bite of his dinner. It was only a matter of minutes before he popped out another question.

"Why does the moon get to stay up when I have to go to bed?"

Quickly covering his amusement over the question, his father ventured an answer for this one. "The moon is the sun's helper, and when the sun has to shine for someone in another part of the world, the moon and the stars take a turn at shining a little light. It's kind of like a night light in your room."

Mr. Jules added graciously, "Children do have a tendency to keep you on your toes, don't they?"

Chapter 21

Startled, Mitch sat up in bed and quickly glanced around the bedroom. In the early morning light, he could faintly see the clock. Six o'clock, time to get up. Stumbling to the bathroom, he splashed water on his face. It had been a fitful night's sleep. Scenes of Marcus, his parents, and Lizzy flashed before him over and over. What had he done? How many lives had his lies and selfishness tainted?

Just yesterday, he had received the letter from Marcus and it lay heavy on his heart. He kept thinking about what it said. *It's never too late to start over. You can take steps to mend the brokenness in your life. How did I get in this mess in the first place, and is there really a way out?*

He made it to work on time, pulling into the lot just a few minutes before seven o'clock. Most of the jobs he had held in the past hadn't lasted this long. Either he had gotten restless and moved to another town to look for work, or his present employer had let him go which usually ended up in his moving on to find another job in another town.

He had been at this job almost two years. It was kind of hard to mess up pumping gas. His age was catching up with him, and he had begun to tire of the frequent moves. He had told so many lies along the way that it was hard to remember who he had told what.

Between the steady stream of customers all day, Mitch did some serious thinking about where he had come from and where he was headed. *How is it that a total stranger walks up to me, asks me a few questions, and I tell him the truth straight away? I guess the truth really wanted to come out and he gave me a chance to come clean. Now what?*

As soon as Mitch got home from work, he scrounged around his place for a piece of paper and sat down to write a letter.

> *Dear Mother and Father,*
>
> *Marcus showed up yesterday at the station where I work. He said he'd met you this summer in his search for me. I guess you were as surprised as I was to meet him. He seems to be a fine young man.*
>
> *Just wanted to let you know I was okay. I'm sorry if I hurt you in any way. Please forgive me.*
>
> *Your son,*
>
> *Mitch*

He folded up the paper and set it by the door to mail from work where he could buy a stamp from his boss.

Marcus was reading some papers in the front room, when his uncle walked in with a worried look on his face.

"Your grandmother Hopkins is in the hospital. One of her neighbors noticed that her living room light had been on all night. They went over to check on her this morning and found her passed out on the couch. I told your mother that we'd be there as soon as we could."

"Let me go grab some things from my room, and I'll be ready to go in a few minutes." On his way back to meet his uncle, Marcus stopped by the kitchen to talk to Kate a minute. They were soon on their way to the hospital.

When they arrived, one look at Lizzy let them know that all was not well. She dabbed at her eyes with her handkerchief as they walked into the room. Her voice quivered as she tried to speak.

"I'm so glad that you're here," she whispered as they embraced her. She was perched on the side of her mother's bed, holding her lifeless hand. Emelia lay still with eyes closed, her chest barely rising and falling with every strained breath.

"What are the doctors saying, Lizzy?"

"They don't expect her to pull out of it." Tears ran down her face. "I'd just like to be able to see her rally one last time to say good-bye."

Marshall walked to the other side of the bed, leaned over, and kissed Emelia on the forehead. He picked up her other hand and held it between his.

"If you can hear me, Emelia, try and squeeze my hand." There was an ever so slight movement, which he acknowledged readily. "We are all here, Emelia," he said gently. "Lizzy, Marcus, and Marshall. You are not alone. We will stay with you till the end." Another slight movement in response.

"Mother, I love you."

"I love you too, Grandmother."

Still holding on to her hands, Marshall and Lizzy looked at each other as they felt one last response. She noticed a tear had rolled down her uncle's cheek. Emelia took one final breath and passed peacefully.

As tears ran down Lizzy's cheeks, she turned to look at Marcus standing behind her. He gently pulled her to her feet and wrapped his arms around her tightly. As she began to sob, she felt his tears moist against her forehead. He leaned down to kiss her on the top of her head.

Marshall leaned over to kiss Emelia one last time on her cheek. The tears flowed freely as he thought back to the day he had kissed Connie for the last time. He joined Marcus and Lizzy, wrapping his arms around them both. This was family...a time to weep...a time to mourn.

As Lizzy slowly regained her composure, Marshall stepped out to the nurses' station to take care of the final paperwork. When he returned to the room, he suggested that they get a bite to eat and then head over to Emelia's house. Lizzy, not wanting to go out any-where, assured them that there would be food at her mother's house.

She fixed some light sandwiches for lunch, enough to satisfy their hunger until they could decide what to do next. By the end of the day, Marshall had made all the funeral arrangements for Thursday afternoon. Not wanting to leave Lizzy by herself, Marshall and Marcus spent the night.

"I'll sleep on the couch tonight," insisted Lizzy. "Uncle Marshall, you take Mother's room, and, Marcus, you can have my old room."

Early the next morning, Marcus contacted his grandparents in Hamilton to let them know about his grandmother's passing. He wasn't sure if this was necessary, but felt it was the polite thing to do. This relationship with this side of the family was still new and he did not want to offend anyone. His grandmother seemed to be the kind of person that would want to know this information.

"I'm not asking you to come to the funeral. That's totally up to you. I just felt like I should let you know."

"Thank you, Marcus. I'm glad you let us know," said his grandfather. "We'll be in touch." There was silence for a minute. "I'm glad you're there for your mother."

This was family too. His thoughts went back to the time when as a young boy. He was alone in a house all by himself. His family had been there all along, but because he really didn't know who he was, he had no way of knowing about them.

He thought about his father and the miserable years he had spent away from his family. What would make a man turn his back on his family? He hoped that the subject of his father would not come up during the next few days. On their drive up the day before, Marcus had shared his concern with his uncle who had agreed to help divert the conversation if there was even a hint of the subject at hand.

"I want to go to Emelia's funeral," insisted Gil when Anna shared the news with him of her passing.

"Are you sure that you're up to it?" Anna questioned.

"No, I'm not sure I'm up to it, but I want to go."

It was rare for Gil to insist on anything, so Anna wanted to honor his request.

"Good morning," Walter said as he set their breakfast tray down in Gil's room.

"Walter, I have a question for you. Do you think that you could help get Gil to Emelia's funeral tomorrow?"

"I'm sure we could fit the wheelchair in the trunk if you can stand the ride," he assured Gil.

"I'd like to try it, if you can help."

"I would be glad to help you. It would be an honor."

"We can take the car," said Anna. "If you drive, there will be just enough room for the five of us, including Ellen and Kate."

Walter thought for a moment. "What if we left right after breakfast in the morning? That way, you can have time to rest at Emelia's house before the funeral in the afternoon."

Anna was relieved. "That's a wonderful idea. Thank you, Walter."

There was a knock on the door about midmorning. When Lizzy opened the door, there was a couple standing there with a covered dish. They introduced themselves, and she invited them inside.

"Emelia was such a lovely lady," said Stuart.

"We will miss her dearly," said his wife, Doris, as she set their casserole down on the table.

"I'm Lizzy, her daughter, and this is my son, Marcus, and my uncle Marshall."

"Let us know if we can do anything for you," they said as they headed for the door. "We live right across the street."

"It was nice to meet you. Thank you so much for coming by and bringing the food," said Lizzy.

The next time there was a knock on the door, Marcus got up to open it.

"Come in," he said as he held the door open for the woman carrying a cake and a plate of muffins.

"Hello, I'm Betty from two doors down, the brown house with green shutters. I'll just set these on the table, dear. I remember you, Lizzy, from when you were a little girl skipping down the sidewalk. Your mother was such a wonderful friend over the years. She always had a good word for everyone. Such a strong woman of faith. And you must be Marcus," she said, turning back around toward him.

"I'll just run along now and get out of your way. It's good to see you again, Marshall. Bye, now," she said as she headed for the door.

"Thank you, Mrs. Blocker," Lizzy called, just as the woman was closing the door behind her.

Lizzy couldn't help but let out a laugh. "Ah, Mrs. Blocker, she can talk faster than anyone I know. Such a sweet lady, though, always checking on Mother and bringing groceries to her. I believe she just set a record for having said the most in such a short time. None of us had a chance to say a word."

Apparently word had spread down the block as a steady stream of neighbors stopped by the house. Each one brought something wonderful to eat and laid it on the table. By lunchtime, there was a feast set out and the delicious aromas were stirring up quite an appetite in all of them.

"Anyone object to eating lunch now?" Marcus asked as he set another casserole down on the dining room table. "This one is from the Holcombs, red brick house at the end of the street."

Lizzy set out plates, silverware, and drinks for all of them as they gathered at the table. "Uncle Marshall, would you give thanks before we eat?" Lizzy asked.

"All of this set before us is a testimony of your mother's legacy of caring and sharing with others," he said before they bowed their heads in reverence and gave thanks.

The meal was delicious, and Marcus teased his mother about it.

"Maybe you could ask the neighbors for their recipes?"

"That wouldn't be a bad idea, Marcus. I could ask them in my thank you notes. Good thinking."

Sitting at one end of the table, Marshall listened to the light-hearted conversation between Lizzy and Marcus. It wasn't that long ago when there was no relationship at all. Several years of diligent healing had brought about a whole new family for Marshall and for them. Family is worth all the pain when love brings them back in.

Instead of sleeping in on his day off, Mitch got up at the regular time and got dressed in the nicest clothes he could find in his closet. Most of the time he just wore work clothes. There was no reason to look nice as he never went anywhere on his days off.

Today was different. He had made the decision to go see his parents. Marcus had challenged him to make amends and make something of his life before it was too late.

Catching a glimpse of himself in the mirror, he stopped to comb his hair and straightened his shoulders. He was tall and lanky to start with and this made him look even taller. The drive to Hamilton went faster than he'd thought. His plan was to go straight to the repair shop and catch his father at work.

He pulled up past the familiar storefront and parked a short distance away. Taking a deep breath, he sat there a moment before getting out of the car. His heart was pounding so hard, he was sure it showed outwardly. Even in the cool crisp air, sweat was beginning to form around his hairline.

You can do this. You can do this. Be strong. You can do this.

He reached for the door and opened it slowly. The bell at the top of the door announced his arrival. As he stepped inside, he glanced around at the array of things in various stages of disrepair.

No lack of business here, he thought to himself. This was the moment. He saw his father walking to the front of the store.

"What can I help you with today?" he said before looking up.

"I was hoping that I could ask for your forgiveness," Mitch managed to say.

His father stopped and stood speechless with his mouth half open.

"Mitch?" he said as he slowly regained his composure and found his voice. "We got your letter, son. Thank you for letting us know that you were okay." He took a step forward, and Mitch matched his step. The two of them gave each other an awkward hug.

"Are you here for the funeral?" his father asked.

"Funeral?" Mitch said with a look of surprise and bewilderment. "Thursday is my day off, and I took a chance that you would be here if I came unannounced."

His father sighed and raised his eyebrows. "I guess you don't know about Mrs. Hopkins. Lizzy's mother passed away two days ago, and her funeral is this afternoon in Shadowbrook. Your mother and I were planning on going to support Marcus and pay our respects to Mrs. Hopkins, even though we never met her."

"Oh," said Mitch nervously. "I guess I've come at a bad time."

"No. No, perhaps this is a good time. I was planning to close the shop at noon." Looking at his watch, he said, "Why don't you go on to the house and see your mother? I should be there in about an hour. I've got a few things to try and finish up here."

"I see you have quite a bit of work here. Is there anything I can help you with?"

"If you're serious, yes, I could use some help in the back."

Mitch followed his father back to the workroom.

"These chairs over here," he said as he pointed to three matching chairs, "have broken rungs that need to be replaced. If you could unscrew these legs, I have the new rungs ready to go in and then the legs can be put back in place."

Mitch picked up a screwdriver and got right to work on the chairs.

"While you work on those, I'll try to get the seat on this rocking chair replaced."

It wasn't so awkward when they each had something to do. After an over twenty-year absence, it was hard to know how to start a conversation. James wished Evelyn was here. She was the talker in the family. She would have known what to say. A painful period of silence passed before he gathered the courage to speak up.

"So, son, how have you been?"

"I've been better, and I've been worse. It's all in how you look at it."

"What do you think about having a son?"

"He seems to be a fine young man with a good head on his shoulders. He really knows how to shake up your life, doesn't he?"

"Yes, he does. He really caught your mother and me off guard as well. He just showed up one day at the shop, kind of like you did today. He said he was looking for you but didn't say who he was. It wasn't until he wrote us a letter that he told us who he was. I'm glad that he came into our lives."

"I'm glad that he came into my life too, even if it was just so I'd come make peace with you and Mother. I really don't know how to relate to him. I wasn't much of a son to you at that age. He has me at a definite disadvantage. I haven't contacted him since he showed up that day about three weeks ago. I don't really know what to say."

"I know what you mean. He and your mother usually do most of the talking."

It felt very strange to be working in the repair shop with his father, especially talking about his son. He still wasn't used to the fact that he even had a son.

With both of them working on the chairs, all but the rocking chair was finished by noon. His father left a note on the door about closing early and then locked up the shop. Mitch drove his car, following his father home. They walked into the house together.

"Evelyn."

"Yes, dear," she said, turning around. "Oh…oh my… Mitch?" Her voice faltered as she stopped what she was doing and greeted her son with a hug. Tears ran down her cheeks as she held him close.

Mitch, surprised by his own emotions, reached up to wipe his own tears away.

His mother stepped back. "Let me look at you. It was so good to hear from you, Mitch, to know that you were okay. And now, to see you too. What a wonderful surprise!"

She quickly added another place setting to the table and filled their bowls with steaming homemade vegetable soup. The cornbread had just come out of the oven. While it was still hot, she cut it into big squares and placed them in a basket covered by a cloth to keep them warm.

"Let's eat while it's hot," she said as they all sat down at the dining room table.

Chapter 22

"Here, put this sweater on, Gil. It's chilly outside, and this will help keep you warm," encouraged his sister.

Walter brought the car around to the front and then went in to get Gil. Anna was helping him put his jacket on when Walter appeared in the doorway.

"Is everybody ready?" he said cheerfully.

"Let me grab my coat, and I'll be ready," said Anna as she quickly slipped it on and grabbed her purse.

"Why don't you bring along a pillow and a blanket, just in case we need them?" he suggested to Anna as he wheeled Gil down the hallway to the front door. Walter had strategically placed several long boards on the front steps to create a makeshift ramp to ease the wheelchair down to the ground. He helped Gil into the front seat where he would have plenty of room to stretch out if need be. Ellen, Kate, and Anna climbed into the back seat, and they headed to Shadowbrook.

"It feels good to get into a car and go somewhere for a change," said Gil. "The last place I went was Marcus's graduation. I'm very thankful that I got to go." He turned to Walter. "I'm very thankful for you as well. From what I've seen and heard, you're doing a wonderful job."

"Mr. Jules says that whoever works at Haleub Place becomes part of the family, and that means you, Walter," chimed in Anna from the backseat.

"Thank you. Thank you both very much. I'm honored," he replied.

Many of the trees they passed had already dropped their leaves as it was the first week of November. The sun was shining bright and the air was still. It was a beautiful day in spite of the reason they were traveling.

Anna, Ellen, and Kate chattered along in the back seat while Walter and Gil said an occasional word to each other. After the first hour, Walter noticed Gil nodding a bit and suggested he use the pillow to prop his head up. With no protest, he picked up the pillow on the seat beside him and placed it under his head against the door. Soon he was snoozing and stayed asleep for the rest of the trip.

They pulled up to Emelia's house, and the cease of motion, plus the opening of car doors was enough to rouse Gil from his slumber. The ladies got out of the car as Walter was getting the wheelchair out of the trunk.

From inside the house, Marshall, Marcus, and Lizzy heard the car doors shutting and came outside to greet them. There was much embracing among them all and an outpouring of condolences as well. Marcus helped Walter get Gil settled in the wheelchair and after wheeling him up the sidewalk, they both lifted him up the few steps on to the porch.

"Come in, come in," said Lizzy. "Make yourselves at home. You're just in time for lunch, and there is plenty for everybody. The neighbors have been so good to bring a steady stream of food."

Marshall placed his arm around Walter's shoulders. "Thank you for being the driver and helping out at this time. I, we, really appreciate it. I hope you are beginning to feel like one of the family by now."

"Yes, I am. You all have been so gracious to include me. This is what families do. They stick by one another and help each other out."

Prior to their arrival, Lizzy had set out eight place settings around the table. They had pulled together seven chairs from around the house, leaving one space for Gil's wheelchair.

"Let me help you get lunch together," offered Ellen as Lizzy began to pull a variety of dishes out of the refrigerator.

"Thank you, Ellen. There are some things already heated up in the oven as well."

Kate, eager to be of assistance offered her help as well.

"If you could fill up the glasses that would be a great help!" called Lizzy over her shoulder.

It wasn't long before all the food was ready and set out on the table.

"Everything's ready," called Ellen to the ones sitting in the living room. "Come on in to the table while it's hot!"

"This sure smells wonderful!" said Walter as he caught a whiff of the aroma in the dining room as he wheeled Gil to the table.

"Mmmm," agreed Gil. "It's so good to be at the table with everyone."

Marshall offered thanks for food and family and the many dishes of food began to be passed around the table until their plates could hold no more.

"Remember," announced Lizzy, "to save room for dessert. We have an assortment of pies and cakes."

Though the occasion was sorrowful, there was joy around the table. Emelia would have been so blessed to know that everyone had gathered there at her home one final time in her honor.

After lunch, Lizzy showed both Anna and Gil a bedroom where each could lay down and rest undisturbed for a while before they had to be at the funeral home.

Evelyn was so surprised by Mitch's surprise visit that she didn't quite know what to say.

"Mother, the soup and cornbread are delicious."

"Thank you, son. It's so good to see you again."

"He showed up at the shop this morning and helped out doing some repairs before we closed the shop early and came home for lunch. What do you think about him riding with us to the funeral? That is, if you want to?" he addressed Mitch. "We could go in at the last minute after the family is seated and sit in the back so no one would notice us."

Mitch and his mother were both silent for a few minutes trying to think through the situation. Mitch was the first to break the silence.

"I guess this could be an opportunity to show up by paying my respects to Lizzy's mother. I wouldn't really have to do much talking, especially if I hung out in the background with both of you. What do you think, Mother?"

"I don't know for sure. You can just slip in and out as nobody will know who you are except Marcus and

Lizzy. It seems to be no coincidence that you show up on the day of Mrs. Hopkins's funeral knowing nothing at all about the situation. I'm sure Marcus will appreciate your coming. It will probably be hard on Lizzy, but then it would probably be hard on her seeing you at any time, no matter the circumstances. At least today, she will be surrounded by family to support her."

James nodded his head as she spoke. He knew his wife would make sense out of the situation. They would do this together as a family.

The funeral wasn't until 3:30 p.m., but the family needed to be there by 2:30 p.m.

"We can trade cars," suggested Marshall to Walter, "and you can bring Gil and Anna a little later.

Gil insisted on going early with everyone else. "I rested in the car on the way up and again at the house. That should be enough, don't you think?" No one wanted to disagree with him, so they all left at the same time.

As the family entered the funeral home, they were touched by the vast array of beautiful plants and flowers that had been sent to honor Emelia. Marshall and Marcus never left Lizzy's side as a steady stream of people stood in line to pay their last respects. Many of them related to Lizzy, countless acts of kindness that her mother had shown to them or someone they knew.

"What a legacy she's leaving behind," remarked Lizzy to her uncle.

"She was a wonderful lady, just like her sister, Connie."

"You must really miss Connie."

"I do, sometimes more than others, especially on occasions like these."

As the time neared for the service to start, Lizzy, Marshall, and Marcus were ushered to their seats. The others had seated themselves earlier, and a chair had been removed at the end of the row to accommodate Gil's wheelchair. Before sitting down, Marcus took one last sweeping glance at the assembly of those who had gathered to honor his grandmother. In the corner of his eye, he saw his grandfather standing at the door, most likely waiting for his grandmother to sign the book. Marcus nodded his head toward him to acknowledge his presence, and he returned the nod. He sighed gently as he took his seat on the end of the row next to his mother.

After several soothing instrumentals, a white-haired elderly gentleman rose from his seat and came forward to deliver the eulogy.

"Few of us realize the importance of people in our lives, until they are gone. It is the precious connection with people that brings meaning and purpose to our lives. So many times, we take for granted those who nurtured us and stood by us as our selfish desires turned our heads to follow the path to pleasure.

"Emelia loved people, especially children. She valued them and made them feel special. She saw the value in each one of us and was always the encourager. Life dealt her various hardships, but she was never one to complain about anything. Perhaps we all could benefit from doing the same.

"Each one of us here today has something she doesn't—another chance to make a difference. Each one of us can influence someone positively or negatively. We can follow our own selfish path to worldly pleasure or we can make a positive impact on someone by simply taking the time to encourage them.

"Life is too short to harbor bitterness, anger, or unforgiveness. Don't take it to the grave with you; let it go. Are you ready to meet your Maker, or do you have some unfinished business to take care of? If you've made mistakes, like we all have, say you're sorry, make amends and move forward. It's built into our nature as humans to heal from wounds. Who of us hasn't had a cut or a scratch and watched the incredible power of healing come from somewhere within our bodies to make our skin as good as new. Healing can also take place within our thoughts, emotions, and relationships.

"With her love and understanding, Emelia touched our lives and made each of us a better person for knowing her. We will miss her kind words, her gentle touch, her beautiful smile, but her legacy can live on as we invest in others what she invested in us. She is laid to rest, but we still have today. Life is precious, invest it wisely.

"Before you leave today, take the time to say a good word to someone. Find someone to share a smile with, give a hug, or encourage in some way. Let this be the beginning of your legacy, your mark on the world. Leave fingerprints of grace."

As the man stepped away from the front, a beautiful instrumental melody began to fill the room. On the way back to his seat, he stopped to shake hands with and encourage each one sitting in the row of family, from Marcus all the way down to Gil. As soon as he sat down, Marcus, Marshall, and Walter stood and took their place along with the other pallbearers to carry the casket down the aisle and out to the hearse. When they returned, the family stood to walk down the center aisle. Lizzy held on to her uncle's arm as they led the way. Marcus followed with Kate, Anna with Gil, and Ellen with Walter as he pushed Gil's wheelchair from behind.

Through her tears, Lizzy saw a sea of faces as she tried not to look at anyone in particular. Uncle Marshall helped her make it to the car where she quickly took refuge inside to regain her composure.

"Kate," Marcus said as soon as they stepped outside the funeral home. "My grandparents are here. I saw them come in just as I was sitting down before the service. Let's go find them to say hello."

Marcus took her hand and led her around to the side entrance hoping to get in behind the crowd that was exiting through the front door. Kate spotted them first.

"Over there." She pointed.

Marcus froze for a minute as he recognized his father standing there with them.

"My father's here, Kate."

"Oh," was all she said as they made their way through the crowd.

Chapter 23

The graveside service ended, and those who were sitting under the canopy, rose to step out onto the grass. Many stood milling about, taking to heart the challenge given to connect with others in a positive way.

Marcus, with Kate by his side, approached his mother who was standing holding on to her uncle's arm.

"Mr. and Mrs. Williams are here if you'd like to meet them."

"Yes, I would," she said as she took a deep breath. "How nice of them to come."

He motioned to them to come over to where they were standing.

"Mother, I'd like you to meet James and Evelyn Williams." They reached out to shake hands with each other. "And this is my uncle, Marshall Jules."

"It's nice to meet you both," Lizzy said. "Thank you so much for coming."

"Yes, it's good to meet you," Marshall said as he shook hands with them as well. "Marcus speaks highly of you both. I'm so glad you have connected with each other."

"We have really enjoyed getting to know Marcus over these past few months, and now, Kate, as well," Evelyn said as she smiled at Kate.

"Please, come visit us at Haleub Place sometime," Marshall offered. "We have several guest rooms, if you'd like to stay overnight."

"Thank you, perhaps we'll take you up on that sometime," she replied. Shooting a quick glance at Marcus, there was an awkward silence as if she meant to say something more.

Marcus cleared his throat and addressed his mother. "There's something I never got the chance to tell you. A few weeks ago, one of Uncle Marshall's business associates handed him Mitch's address, which he in turn handed to me. I went to check it out that day and met my father."

At this news, Lizzy gasped and reached for her uncle's arm to steady her.

"Mitch sent us a letter," added Evelyn, "telling us that Marcus had showed up and introduced himself. He told us he was okay and then asked our forgiveness for any way he had hurt us in the past. We were as shocked as you are today."

Lizzy stood there silent, not knowing what to say or how to respond.

"On a whim, Mitch showed up at the shop today," James continued. "He knew nothing of your mother's passing, and we had already made plans to come to the funeral. He came with us today and is standing over there under that tree," he said as he pointed in his direction. "He wasn't sure if you would want to see him, especially today, but he sends his condolences and says that he's sorry he never met her."

Stunned, Lizzy turned her head in his direction and stared. She recognized his silhouette, but something was different about it. His former confident posture had been replaced by sagging shoulders and a nervous stance. What had he become? Where was the old Mitch she had known and loved at one time?

He caught her glance and nodded his head slightly as he raised a hand halfway to acknowledge her. She nodded ever so slightly and then looked away.

"We'd better be going now," Evelyn spoke up. "It was nice to have met you. I hope this didn't upset you too much, especially today."

Not able to find any words, Lizzy smiled weakly and nodded.

"Let me walk you to your car," Marcus offered as they turned to leave. He and Kate walked with them as Mitch started walking to meet them at the car.

"How did she take it?" asked Mitch when he caught up with them.

"She's pretty much in shock right now," Marcus answered. "It's been a hard day for her anyway because of her mother. Perhaps you could write her a letter. Here," he said as he handed his father one of his business cards with her address written on the back of it. "Be honest with her. No more lies." They both stood there for a moment, not knowing what to say next. "Thank you for coming today," Marcus said as he reached out and gave his father a hug.

"Thank you for taking the time to look for me, Marcus. It's good to see you again."

Marcus and Kate hugged his grandparents good-bye and then stood there watching them drive away. As they headed back toward his mother and uncle, Walter approached them.

"Kate, we're about ready to head back to Haleub Place. It's been a long day for everyone, especially Gil, and we need to get him back home soon."

"Sure, I'll be with you in a few minutes," she said as she turned to Marcus.

"I'm so thankful that you were here with me today," Marcus said as he put his arm around her shoulders. "I should be home sometime tomorrow. We'll stay here with Mother tonight. Kate, I love you and I'll miss you until tomorrow." He leaned over to kiss her on the top of her head.

Looking into his eyes, Kate whispered, "I love you too, Marcus. I'll see you tomorrow."

She walked over to give Lizzy a hug good-bye. Mr. Jules gave Kate a hug as well.

"Thank you for being a part of our family, Kate," he said with a twinkle in his eye. Pointing to Walter and the others, he said, "They've already said their good-byes and are waiting for you in the car. Have a safe trip home."

"We will," she called over her shoulder as she headed to the car.

"Let's head back to the house," Marshall suggested to Lizzy and Marcus. "It's been a long day for all of us."

"That sounds good to me," agreed Marcus.

"Me too," chimed in Lizzy.

They all got in the car, and Marcus drove them through the cemetery. Lizzy looked out the window and sighed.

"They're both finally at rest together, side by side. May they rest in peace."

"How are you holding up?" Walter asked as he glanced over at Gil.

"I'm a bit tired, but I'm doing all right. I might snooze a bit on the way home."

"I'd expect you to," he replied.

"Who was the older couple that Marcus introduced to his mother and Mr. Jules?" Anna asked Kate.

"They are Marcus's grandparents, James and Evelyn Williams."

"That was nice of them to come," said Ellen.

"Yes, it was," agreed Kate. "Did you happen to notice a tall, thin man standing under a tree by himself?"

"There were so many people, I didn't notice," said her mother.

"Well, if you had noticed, then you would have seen Marcus's father, Mitch Williams. I met him at the funeral home before we went to the cemetery."

"His father came to the funeral?" Anna said in amazement. "What did Lizzy say when she saw him?"

"She didn't say anything. She was pretty shocked and just nodded at him."

"What a day," Ellen exclaimed. "She must be exhausted with all of this happening on the same day as her mother's funeral."

"The poor dear," Anna declared, shaking her head.

James was the first to speak as they drove out of the cemetery. "I'm glad we all came today. It was a bit awkward but a perfect opportunity for a brief meeting of families."

Evelyn joined in. "It was good to meet everyone, especially Lizzy. I think Marcus may have a good suggestion, if you want to connect at all with Lizzy, a letter would probably be the best option. Even if you don't want to connect with her, a letter of apology or explanation would be a good way to bring closure to both of you."

"I'm new at this forgiveness thing, but you're right, it does bring closure to open wounds and unanswered questions. It's a relief to be able to talk to you both again after all these years. I'm sure it's a relief to Marcus to have found his father even though I may be a disappointment to him. At least he knows the truth now. As to Lizzy, I'm not exactly sure that I know how I feel about her. Come to think of it, I suppose, technically we're still married which could limit her options for the future."

"Give yourself some time to sort all this out," his mother suggested. "We all have come a long way today by just making connections with everybody." Changing the subject, she asked, "Can you stay the night, or do you have to drive back tonight?"

"I have to get back tonight so I can be at work by seven in the morning."

"If you don't mind, I can heat up the soup from lunch when we get home, and you can eat before you have to start back."

"Thanks, that sounds good. Thank you also for not asking me a lot of questions today. I know I owe you and others a lot of explanations, but today didn't seem to be the right time for focusing on me. It was time to focus on somebody else for a change."

"Why didn't you mention to me anything about finding your father?" Lizzy asked Marcus as they sat down at the table to eat dinner.

"I'm not sure why. I guess I was hoping to hear something from him or at least that he had contacted his parents. I wanted him to have the option of making the first move on his own. I didn't foresee a situation like today coming up so suddenly.

"With Grandmother in the hospital and then her passing, it didn't seem to be a good time to bring it up. There was no way I or his parents would have known that he would show up today of all days. I know it was a shock to you, but it all happened so fast, there was no way to prepare you for it."

Lizzy ate a few bites of her dinner before she responded.

"It was a shock to see him without warning, but he didn't catch me off guard. With you and Uncle Marshall searching for him, I knew there was a definite possibility that he might turn up at any time. I was not expecting him today, but at least with everything else going on, it was only a small dose of him.

"I didn't have to speak to him, and I'm not really in a position where I have to respond in any way. At least now I have a chance to think ahead in case he shows up again or tries to make contact in the future."

"I'm glad you see it that way, Lizzy," said her uncle. Turning his head toward Marcus, he said, "It was nice to meet Mr. and Mrs. Williams."

"I'm glad you both got to meet them. They really are nice people."

Ellen put together a quick dinner as soon as they got home. Walter carried the tray down to Gil's room and then joined Kate and Ellen at the kitchen table.

"It's been a long, full day for everyone," said Walter. "I think I'll turn in early tonight. "I'll be surprised if Gil and Anna are still up when I go back for their tray in a little while."

"Thanks for lunch and dinner," said Mitch as he rose from the table. "It was good to spend the day with you both. I'd better get on the road. I'll be in touch."

His parents both rose from the table and hugged him good-bye. He let himself out and closed the door behind him. A sigh of relief escaped him as he heard the door click behind him. *That wasn't as hard as I thought it would be.*

All the way home, he replayed the events of the day in his mind. How strange to be in his father's shop again, to be in their home again. He hadn't even taken the time to go look at his old room. There were too many memories stirred up in one day.

What a sobering experience to unexpectedly find himself at a funeral, at a gravesite. The words from the funeral echoed in his mind about forgiveness, about leaving a legacy, about realizing too late the importance of people in one's life.

It would take some time to sort all this out in his mind. He was glad he had to work the next day because if left to himself, he would probably just sit and stare into space. Too much time on his hands was not a good thing right now. It was late when he got home, and he went straight to bed hoping sleep would come quickly to turn off all these thoughts, at least for tonight.

Kate and Ellen had the evening to themselves as everyone else was either away or had already gone to bed. Kate gathered her courage to ask some questions that had been on her mind a long time.

"Mother, since Marcus found his father, I've been thinking a lot lately about my father as well. I don't remember much about him, and you never talk about him. Do you feel like talking about him?"

Ellen was silent a moment before answering.

"I'm sorry, Kate. It was so hard to work through losing him. I tried not to talk about him thinking it would make you sad if I kept reminding you about him. I guess I went too far in never bringing him up at all. Of course, you would want to know about your father. Forgive me for not ever mentioning him around you."

She walked over to the closet and took down a box off the top shelf.

"I don't have too many pictures of him, but I do have a few."

She handed the box to her daughter who gingerly opened it and began to lift out, one by one, pictures and cards he and her mother had given each other over the years. Kate glanced up at her mother to see her reaction and saw her wipe away a few tears that had rolled down her cheeks.

"I'm sorry, Mother, if I've upset you by asking about him."

"No, no. These are good tears. I should have shared these things with you a long time ago. Perhaps it will do us both good to talk about him. I've had all this bottled up for years, and you've had all these questions on your heart. It's long overdue that we have this time together. Ask me anything you want. It will be a good release for both of us."

Chapter 24

Several weeks had passed since Emelia's funeral. Lizzy had to get back to work, and Marcus and Uncle Marshall had helped her close up the house until a decision could be made about what to do with it. She missed her mother's company, their time together, the cooking lessons, and their heart-to-heart talks. The holidays were just around the corner, and Christmas wouldn't be the same without her.

There were hints from Marcus leading Lizzy to believe that perhaps an engagement ring might be in store for Kate this Christmas. She was excited about their prospects for the future, but at the same time, it was a reminder to her of her singleness. Over the years she had discouraged anyone from taking an interest in her by simply stating that she was married.

So, am I married or not? Now that Mitch has surfaced, it would be nice to know one way or another. Time is slipping by, and I'm not getting any younger. Do I keep waiting, or should I make the first move to closure of some sort?

Christmas at Haleub Place was a wonderful time. The decorations were simple, but beautiful, and the food was beyond compare. There were always guests stopping by, even houseguests from time to time. With the consent of his mother, Marcus had invited his grandparents to come and stay at Haleub Place for Christmas. They had accepted his invitation on the grounds that if Mitch decided to come see them, they would stay home with him. Lizzy felt better knowing this, but Mitch was still unpredictable and there was no guard against an impromptu appearance.

Uncle Marshall had been a good sounding board for her as she tried to sort through the facts versus her emotions. Every angle offered its own unique challenges and possibilities. Ultimately, it was up to Lizzy to continue as is or to make a move of some sort. Whatever she chose to do, or not to do, she would have to rest in that decision without murmuring or complaining about its outcome. She would have to be at peace with herself no matter what.

"Anna, it looks like I'm going to make it. There was a time there when I wondered if I would ever see another Christmas."

"I'm glad you're still here, Gil. I would have missed you terribly."

"I'm glad you slowed down too, Anna, or you might have found yourself in the same condition I'm in."

"It worked out nicely for us to have Walter and Kate take over for us, Gil. Walter needed a home and Haleub Place needed Walter. Kate's been family all along anyway, but it looks like she may be even *more* family soon."

"How can she be *more* family than she already is, Anna?"

"She and Marcus are a lot more than just friends now, Gil—if you get the picture."

"I get the picture, Anna. They'll be good for each other."

"Have you noticed how Ellen and Walter look at each other? I think there might be something more brewing there too."

"Now, Anna, don't get carried away with all your matchmaking thoughts."

"I'm not getting carried away. I've watched how they interact with each other."

"Next, you'll be telling me that Lizzy and Mitch are back together," he said, shaking his head.

"Now, Gil, I'm not going that far. Lord only knows what will happen with those two, if anything happens with those two. That's a hard one to unravel."

She sat silent for a few minutes. A slight creaking sound could be heard from her chair as she rocked back and forth while gazing out the window.

"Gil, do you ever wish that you had married?"

"To whom, Anna?"

"Oh, anyone that struck your fancy."

"No one ever struck my fancy, Anna," he said, chuckling lightly. "What about you? Do you ever wish that you had married?"

"No one ever asked me, Gil."

"I'm not sure you would have stood still long enough for anyone to ask you, Anna," he said teasingly.

"I would throw this pillow at you for saying that, if there wasn't a hint of truth in what you're saying," she said, trying to hide a smile. "My only regret is not having any children to carry on for us."

"We've got Kate and Marcus," he piped up. "They're as good as children. They're family anyway."

"You're right, Gil. I do feel like we had a hand in raising them. I don't know if I feel like a parent or a grandparent."

"Does it matter, Anna? It's the relationship that really counts, not the title."

"You're right, Gil. You're right."

"Uncle Marshall, I was wondering if you could help me out with something?"

"What did you have in mind, Marcus?"

"Is there any way we could invite Kate's grandparents for Christmas without her finding out? I know she gets to see her mother's parents from time to time, but I'm talking about the Silvertons, on her father's side."

"That shouldn't be too hard to do. I can get their address for you, if you'd like to write to them and ask."

"Thanks, I'd really appreciate that. I knew you could help," he said with a twinkle in his eye.

"Are you up to something, Marcus?"

"Maybe. You'll just have to wait and see, won't you?" he said, teasingly.

Marshall laughed. "Christmas is a time for surprises, isn't it?"

It felt like it was getting colder every day. The light snow from the night before was not melting on this overcast breezy morning. Between customers, Mitch took shelter in the shop to warm his hands and feet. A double pair of socks, a scarf wrapped around his neck, a heavy-hooded jacket, and a pair of gloves was not enough to keep him warm. It was days like today that made him stop and wonder about what he was doing with his life.

He had not been in touch with anybody since that day he had shown up at Mrs. Hopkins's funeral. It sounded good that he should write a letter to Lizzy, but he had no idea what to say. He didn't know what to say to Marcus or his own parents, much less, Lizzy. Even though he was married to Lizzy, he wasn't sure how he felt about her or how she felt about him. He had no idea of how to be a father to a grown son and almost felt like Marcus was the father and he was the son. Living four hours away from anybody posed a problem of its own, especially only having Thursdays and Sundays off from work.

It was easier to not do anything than to decide what to do. The only problem with not doing anything was that all this had been gnawing on him inside ever since Marcus had showed up that day at work. If he were to have a relationship with anybody, it meant possibly relocating and finding another job. Lately, his mind had been drifting back to the day he had helped his father out at the shop. There was plenty of work there, no shortage of repairs to be done.

He had never asked for any days off before. He had never had a reason to ask off. Right before closing time that night, Mitch walked over to his boss.

"I was wondering if I could take off a few days around Christmas? If not, that's okay, but I just thought that I would ask."

"Let me talk to Wilson first to see if he can cover for you. I'll let you know after I talk to him tomorrow."

"Thank you, sir. I appreciate it. I'll see you in the morning."

"Good night, Mitch."

"It will be nice to spend Christmas this year with family," Evelyn remarked to her husband as they were sitting in their living room. "Who would have thought, at this time last year, that this Christmas would be any different than all the others. Sometimes things can be so close to you, but you don't even know they're there until your eyes are opened to see them."

"Marcus has opened our lives, hasn't he? Kate's a real sweet girl. It wouldn't surprise me if they got married. What do you think, Evelyn?"

"I think you're right, James. Not only did we get Marcus as a grandson, but he brought along Lizzy and Kate and even opened a pathway to Mitch. Mr. Jules seems to be a very nice man as well. Then there's Mr. Wagner and the Thompsons and Kate's mother, Mrs. Silverton. At this point, it wouldn't even surprise me if your brother, Nicholas, showed up out of the blue."

James chuckled. "That would be a surprise, wouldn't it? You know, as fast as things have been happening in the last few months, it's almost as if I'm expecting things to happen. I've got hope again. Instead of expecting the same things day after day, I'm meeting each new day looking for what new surprise could happen. It's kind of exciting when you don't know what's going to happen next."

"James, I haven't seen this much life in you in years. You're becoming a bit unpredictable yourself," she said, laughing.

He smiled as he sat up in his easy chair with a twinkle in his eye.

"Evelyn," he said, patting his knee.

"Why, James, it's been years since you—"

"Evelyn," he interrupted as he cocked his head to one side and winked at her.

Evelyn got up from the couch and wiped her eyes. She walked over to her husband and gently sat in his lap as he pulled her close. He hadn't held her like this in years. It felt good to be in the arms of someone who loved her.

Lizzy packed her bag and headed to the station. She had saved up enough vacation time at work to be able to take off a full week at Christmas. Tucked under one arm, she carried the portfolio of all the drawings she had been working on for weeks to give as Christmas gifts.

She sat down in her seat, took a deep breath, and let out an audible sigh. Just this week, she had made her decision about Mitch. Settled in her mind, she was determined not to waver from it. *Be strong, Lizzy. You can do it. Don't look back. Keep moving forward. Keep walking.*

At the next stop, a woman got on the train and sat down in the empty seat beside her. She turned to face Lizzy, and they exchanged smiles.

"Is that you, Lizzy? Lizzy Hopkins?"

"Yes," said Lizzy slowly as she tried to put a name with the face. "Peggy?" she said in disbelief. "Why, I haven't seen you since graduation. How are you doing? It's good to see you!"

"You too, Lizzy!"

"Where are you headed, Peggy?"

"I'm on my way to my daughter's home for Christmas. And you?"

"I'm going to my uncle's for Christmas. My son is there too. So who did you marry, Peggy? Anyone I know?"

"Michael Taylor. Do you remember him?"

"Yes, I do. Congratulations, a little belated!"

"And you, who did you marry? I lost touch with everybody soon after we graduated."

"Mitch Williams. We got married, but it didn't last long. He left before he knew I was expecting."

"I'm sorry, Lizzy. I know that must have been hard for you raising a son by yourself."

Not wanting to go into too much detail, Lizzy added. "I had help from my mother and my uncle." She was silent for a moment, then continued. "What about Michael? Will he be joining you at your daughter's home?"

"He's tied up with business until the last minute. We decided I would come early and he would meet me as soon as he could. Do you remember Butch and Sammy?"

Lizzy nodded.

"The three of them are all in business together. Butch is not married. We should all get together sometime after the holidays."

Peggy pulled out a scrap of paper and wrote her address on it.

"Here," she said, handing the paper to Lizzy. "After Christmas!"

"Thank you," Lizzy said as she slid the paper into her pocket. "I hope it snows for Christmas," she said, changing the subject.

"Me too," replied Peggy.

They chatted back and forth until Lizzy's stop.

"Have a wonderful Christmas!" Lizzy said as she got up to get off the train. "It was nice to see you again, Peggy."

"It was nice to see you too, Lizzy. Have a very Merry Christmas!"

Lizzy's thoughts were churning as she stepped off the train and waved to Marcus who was waiting for her at the station. Life was full of challenges. Life was unpredictable. Life was good.